T0317980

twelve

twelve

twelve
vanessa jones

Flamingo
An Imprint of HarperCollins*Publishers*

Flamingo
An Imprint of HarperCollins*Publishers*
77–85 Fulham Palace Road,
Hammersmith, London w6 8jb

www.harpercollins.co.uk

Published by Flamingo 2000

A catalogue record for this book
is available from the British Library

ISBN 978-0-00-655194-2

Photograph of Vanessa Jones © Tony Davis 2000

For Joyce and Noël

one

Every Friday night we rehearse the desertion of the city. Its pull becomes a push – a heartbeat pumping us out – to its limits and beyond. Trouble is we've got varicose veins. Or gout – look at this road. Stasis. We're always stuck on this spooky bit of road, and it is always the same. Once it must have been a normal slice of quiet suburbia, but now most of the houses are boarded up: sold to the department of transport, bought by the department of road expansion, leased to the drivers of these cars.

One resident in every ten is hanging on. And they have painted their cause on the boards of their neighbours, their rantings against the drivers and their exhausts, dirt, noise. But I have only ever seen this in evidence and never the protesters themselves. 'Time is suspended here,' I say to Edward, who's driving. 'The anti-car campaigners always in precisely this state of invisible outrage, the cars in exactly this state of non-movement.' Every moment is a freeze-frame in an action movie – it is a sculpture, a still life.

He doesn't answer because he's considering his next

move in a word game we're playing, a meaningless game, the way to win it is not to come to the end of it, its only point is to pass the time. 'How apt,' I think, and laugh. I say 'Everything's a metaphor,' and then, '– I love statements like that which prove your point.'

Edward says, 'You talk absolute shit, do you know that, Lily?'

'The car is the city's metaphor for freedom,' I say, 'its get-out clause' – but once in, freedom is lost. We have no choice but to go with this not-so flow. Breathing in. People use this gas to kill themselves!

'T-H-M,' says Edward.

Country weekends. Weekends away. 'I'm going away for the weekend.' Maybe one day no one will live in the country. Perhaps one day it will be populated only from Friday evenings till Monday mornings and the city in hush.

'Your go,' says Edward. 'God, this is boring.'

'Well, we could have a conversation.'

'Fine,' he says. 'You start.'

Edward and I are friends. We are better friends in theory than in practice. I love him, but what does that mean? We are going to his parents' house, which is my favourite house – I love it and I like to think I have an understanding with it. It is elegant and grand, it is family and snug. How? Every room I want to breathe-in. I am always given the same bedroom, which I call Lily's Room, but Edward's family call it Bobbin's room after some great aunt who lived there once. It feels like home to me but it is not my home, and I do not belong to it.

When we arrive, we'll see through the window Edward's parents sitting at the table in the middle of the kitchen. If you go in through the back door (and I have never been in through the front), the first room you come to is the kitchen. It is dark, in the way that a wood is dark. We'll leave our bags in the car. We'll walk in looking exhausted and dirty in the way parents expect, and secretly like. Edward's mum will make room for us at the table. She'll jump up and try to fetch us things, and Edward and his dad will tell her to sit back down. Then the others will arrive and there'll be a general commotion involving luggage and kisses and fragments of lives. There'll be a massive lasagne for supper and a treacle tart and after Edward's parents have gone to bed, we'll go into the drawing room and drink coffee, and take drugs.

I often wonder how much our parents would like us if they knew the whole truth.

Edward has quite an odd collection of friends which he likes to mix and match on these weekends. And although some of them look like they're mutual, really I only see them these days by proxy, when I'm with him. We look uncomfortable in the drawing room. We are neither old enough nor young enough to own it. We look like props on the over-stuffed sofas, smugly smoking our joints or, now that we all have a bit more money, snorting a surreptitious line of cocaine. We are an uneasy mix of tailored suits and denim jackets. We have almost completely let go our dreams into the i-wish abyss. But not quite. Another year perhaps, two? at most five.

We're never at our best on Friday nights. Something it is about coming to the country. We all invest the 'country' with some sort of healing power, and I don't know whether it actually possesses it, but I do think it's odd that anyone should lead a life they need constant respite from. Tonight I'll go to bed earlier than I have done all week. Tonight I'll sleep in Lily's bed, next to the window which looks out onto fields of sheep. I'll read a few lines of the Agatha Christie novel that's always on the bedside table and listen to the silence. It'll be dark. Properly dark like it is in a memory. No dreams.

After breakfast, before lunch, we go for a walk. To nowhere in particular. Edward's garden becomes fields becomes the whole wide world. It is summer and the trees look heavy. Flowers bud bloom and rot on their stalks – decadence. If Edward's mum had come with us we should have heard the names of them all, but today she doesn't come. Too busy in her usually mysterious way. I've never met a mother who isn't. They make lists, which sometimes branch off into sublists: a, b, c, d. In her absence I ask Edward to name everything. It is another game we play. If he doesn't know, he knows to make it up. I find this delightful, like being a gummy child. Or Eve.

He points out to the others the line of cedars visible from this hill. He has taught me to love cedars – the elegant stillness of their elongated limbs – but weeping beeches are my favourite trees. They look like the sea stopped. There is one in his garden, and sitting under it I get a panoramic view of everyone's calves playing croquet. There are sounds but not the words they are making. I'm wondering what Edward talks about when I'm not there and whether he has the same conversations. The light under here is the same as the light of the kitchen. Hands on mallets on balls. Clock-clock.

He is a fanatic games player, Edward. Chinese checkers, bridge, chess and on rainy days, Risk. I have spent whole weekends watching him try for world domination. He tells me that tonight will be perfect for murder so we bring the dining room outside. Tablecloth, candles, the whole kit and boodle. It is an old crone of a moon. Ace of hearts kills; Jack detects.

Edward says 'the secret of life is to enjoy the world without wanting to possess it' – but not everyone can borrow such an eden. I feel like pointing this out to him as we drive past the high-rises on the way back to town. I don't, because we're having an argument. The same argument we always have on the way back home about me, and how I expect to be driven to my front door. I quite like it because by the time it's over we *have* driven to my front door. Rewind. All return journeys are shorter, like the last half of the week once you've got past the hill of Thursday, 12 p.m.

Tonight Shirley is watering the hollyhock in her front garden. I say garden, but really it is just the space between the road stop and her house start. She planted it out last year and this summer her hollyhock has swollen to gigantic proportions. It really is an extraordinary sight, barely diminished by her presence next to it.

I have discovered that it is a mistake to make friends with your next door neighbours. I can't slide into my house now without having some intercourse with her and tonight I'm just not in the mood. It's the same as going back to school after the long summer holidays. You've got something precious from home in your bag, and suddenly you see your teacher or your best friend and it's sullied. You're back down to earth and it was only a dream – silly. When I get in I'll put a bag of blueberries down, and Edward's mum's chocolate brownies, and they'll seem completely out of place and stupid. I'll go to my room, and it will look like time hasn't passed, like nothing's happened. I can't bear it. I want to hold on for a bit longer before I believe it. 'Put your sunglasses on,' says Edward. I do, I get away with 'Nice weekend?' and 'Yes, thank you.'

At the moment, everything reminds me of being at school. Our individual lives are minute replicas of our whole species' evolution. When a baby gets up onto its two legs it becomes *homo erectus*, becomes *homo sapiens*. Thinking man. It occurred to me at the ends of term that the school was a magnet momentarily switched off scattering us, its iron filings, into the beyond. This is how I feel again on Friday nights when we abandon our city, one day never to return. But which day? We live in the meantime. At school there is that sense of another life that will be yours, and now I sense it too. Home – not far away, but too far to touch.

In the meantime, this is my home. Josh is in the kitchen smoking a cigarette. There are five clean shirts on the table beside him, sunday-evening-newly-ironed. The working week is a steep rock face, and tonight is for laying out our crampons. Tomorrow we'll put on our garb and ointments and we'll leave the tent for the week ahead. Monday morning a little slow, but we're picking up momentum. We're more in the flow by Tuesday: throw the rope, click the clip, up a bit. On Wednesday we can neither see the ground beneath nor the summit above us, we're dangling on Wednesday. Then dragging ourselves up by our fingernails on Thursday and panting at 12 p.m. Thursday afternoon is – the edge of the abyss: the relief, the run towards it, the ground falling away, time accelerating, it's a roller coaster we're on, we're all feeling a little hysterical, silly we somersault towards The Weekend.

Tonight is just the beginning. Tonight I'm not looking forwards, I'm remembering. I'm hanging onto time and willing it to slow down. I kiss Josh's forehead. I take my mementos out of my bag and as I predicted they look vaguely flat and tired. Still. They're still brownies, they're still blueberries and cream, and one of life's treats. Josh and I eat them in the garden with a cup of coffee. He swings his legs up onto the bench so his knees hold his elbows hold his hands hold his head. He says he thinks the most highly-evolved form of life is the jellyfish and wishes he could be one, floating. He is one big sigh Josh, and not always of relief.

In mawkish moments it has always been Josh and me.

Before we met – I don't like to think about it – I couldn't survive it now that I know better. In that respect, perhaps, I'm with God and his adamance on the Tree of Knowledge – once you know things it is very hard to unknow them. It is Josh has created this garden, he insisted on it. He said, in the summer, it's like having a spare room. It is too small for a lawnmower so he put down paving and a step. To cut us off from Shirley on one side and mr faceless on the other he erected a wooden fence that creaks like a ship in the wind. He doesn't believe in buying plants, so from trips to the country, from front yards we passed on the street, from commemorative gardens in town he has ripped cuttings. Usually under cover of darkness, but never intended. His garden has grown exactly as he has grown, slowly and by series of chance. It is the same with all his possessions, furniture, clothes, books and friends. I try to be more like him but I am too much in a hurry. I have an idea and like to realise it all at once. He waits, and he finds the design by accident. He is far less often disappointed.

I don't think I have ever seen the garden looking as real as it does this year. It has come into itself. The plants are growing so thickly that it looks like a secret, but still it manages to steal the sun. In it, on the paving, Josh has drawn a backgammon board in chalk. A game of skill and chance. He suggests one.

Could I ever not understand backgammon? could I survive without Josh? how did people get hold of me before my mobile phone? can we forget concepts once we have them? could we unlearn the word "car"? Luxury turns right turns given turns necessity. When I was younger I could almost have moved in with someone who lived in a barrel of water, but I have definite needs now, definite edges. I don't understand how anyone manages to fall in love after the age of seventeen. I do understand claustrophobia.

Because every day I make the decision to see exclusively. I must not register certain realities – like: there is no silence, or: I am never further than ten feet away from another person above below left right – for I am going down a tunnel. And looking straight ahead it seems there is room to manoeuvre but noticing the backdrop is never starting again, and attempting to turn around is: panic.

Josh and I make packed lunches for each other. It started off as an economy drive but has become a game of surprise. It was his turn last week and on Wednesday he shocked me with a cockle sandwich. It was a coup, not least because he did it on the most uninspiring day of the week. This week it's my go, and I've decided on a radically different approach, five days of egg mayonnaise. It's a huge price for not-that-funny a joke I realise this morning as I'm slicing the bread. For a start, egg mayonnaise first thing. For another, I too have to eat it. For a third, if someone did it to me I'd think they were very sad. Will he? Well . . . ? Here we go.

When we first started working, we used to smoke a joint before we left the house. I don't know how we did it, it is entirely unthinkable now. At the least delay on the under- ground, we'd come home and phone in to say we were catching a bus. We did wonder if they could hear us filling the kettle on the end of the line, but we decided we didn't care – they could sack us – then we'd roll another. Funny how you get over it without noticing. Funny how what the company does was once 'what they do' and is now 'what we do'. Funny how it doesn't hurt.

Still, Monday morning it is definitely them and us and 'them' is everyone apart from me and Josh. We stride to the station, we sandwich ourselves between varying amounts of aliens and we look straight ahead, soft focus.

So many people all rushing to do their jobs. I wish I knew whether they enjoyed them, or got from them some sense of satisfaction. To my mind, work is the most monumental waste of time. I know that I could be thinking a larger thought, or having a more interesting conversation elsewhere. But I suffer from a lack of imagination. I don't know where elsewhere is, or how to make it pay my rent, I can't picture anything that could keep me interested nine-to-five, monday-to-friday, forty-eight-weeks-of-the-year. And I'm inclined to believe that everyone agrees with me for if they didn't, surely there'd be no such word as 'holiday'. Watching them, joining them struggle for space in this survival-of-the-fittest test first thing in the morning, every morning, the city seems to me a complex organism with a terminal disease. The new age has notions which oppose its ethic – fitness, health food, relaxation – and the age of communication has negated its reason to be.

After twenty minutes, Josh goes east and I go west. When I was little, I used to steal application forms and leaflets from banks, and with some other small friend whose every detail is now lost to me, played 'work' which consisted of, fundamentally, filling in these forms and reorganising them in piles. This is pretty much what I find myself doing for real now and it's somewhat lost its appeal. The origami heaps on my desk are exactly how I left them minus my friday-air of elation. As far as they're concerned, the week-end was my illusion.

It is ironic that, as an atheist to the work ethic, I have incarnated as a recruitment consultant. It startles me some-times that my journey to this point is entirely due to a secretarial course that I never wanted to take. If I could unlearn to type, how different my life might have been. I started here as a temporary secretary and I have never left. Well, you've got to do something and I'm no good at first days. On my first day at school I got sent to the corner for colouring the moon in yellow and not knowing why I'd used that colour; I hated being new and I was new often. Now, I'm an old hand and no longer a secretary, in fact I've got one of my own. He tells me this morning that I have wall-to-wall interviews till lunch time. Time will fly then. Then I'll think of Josh, ignorantly tucking in.

Time is subjective. The interviewees sitting in reception find the ten minutes until I can see them an eternity of sweating palms. The fly on the wall beside them spies in an even slower motion which lets it dodge the swiftest of swatting hands. Someone has found life on Mars. Well. Even if it were more than a single-celled bacteria, it would be as distinct from a human as a fly, or a lion. It would have no knowledge of day or night, week weekend, month year century millennium. We have invented millennia. And although I know we've made them up, I can't help but feel apocalyptic at this point in time, in the madness of weekday mornings, on the Friday nights when we abandon our metropolis, one day never to return.

The city is sick. At its centre is chaos because everyone within it is dispensable, yet the central icon of our times is: the individual. In a tunnel though, there is no direction but straight ahead. Evolution involves the collation of information, to no end but survival, but how will we survive? I may feel apocalyptic but I've no idea what should happen next, I suffer a lack of imagination. And so does everyone else, I imagine. We're neither-nor. We laud people over machines, but we can't help looking forward to the day when computers can make love to us. We're unsure whether to live organically farming or safe within the helmet of a virtual world. It is the end of the decade, the century and the millennium. It is Thursday Afternoon all over the world and this is what I'm wondering: where are we going for the weekend?

two

Shirley's father died when she was eleven months old. It is this, she says, that has given her her unique spin on the politics of men and women. 'Being brought up without a father,' she tells us quite often, although now it doesn't grate so, 'gives you a very different outlook. It means you don't play to roles.' She is married to Andrew and together they have a small son called Oliver.

It is because of Oliver that Shirley and I met in the first place. She was background music before then, heavily pregnant when we moved in and leading to a few *do you think they know they're alive?* conversations: babies in stomachs and bodies in general and breast-feeding (it can't be right). But babies, they perform the same function as dogs do in human interaction. You pretend you've not noticed the person queuing next to you for the past three months and then all of a sudden it's 'hello, fella' and 'isn't he sweet?' and 'does he bite?'

This house has Shirley on one side, mr faceless on the other and behind it, garden-to-garden back-to-back, it has naked neighbours. These others have neither children nor animals and so have remained objects of peeking and conjecture. Sometimes sitting in the garden, doing my thing while they are doing theirs, it seems like we are plastic figures placed in toy town being repositioned by a giant child. To him, mr faceless is a secret. He is intriguing because neither Josh nor I are able to describe him. If we saw him somewhere other we'd never recognise him, and we quite often have arguments about the colour of his hair. Our naked neighbours live in a flat parallel with our first floor. On weekday mornings, they iron shirts in their boxer shorts and they eat cereal in them at the weekends. I go red when I see them on the street fully clothed. They have the bodies of young gods and I'm sure that to the child in charge they're superheroes. And me and Josh . . . ?

Shirley, because we spoke, dwells in the realms of bleak reality. She is a constant source of minor irritation. She claims not to play to roles with Andrew, but she has taken to them with a vigour with me. Like her marriage though, I'm sure she views our relationship as evidence to support her theories and, vexingly, I see how she could be justified. Still, there must be degrees of correctness, in the end I must know that I'm more right than she is, otherwise we'd agree.

Not that she knows we disagree. This is one of the things that most annoys me about myself.

I have no idea what Shirley was like before she became a parent, but she so entirely epitomised the last few weeks of pregnancy that I'm sure that she has taken to every stage of her life with like completeness. As soon as she became a mother to Oliver she became a mother to me, and now feels it her duty to advise me on the complicated process of love. This morning she came round to drop off Oliver and dropped off also the benefit of her experience. She said 'No red lipstick today then?'

I said, 'No, I didn't like it, I could feel it on my lips. And anyway Josh told me I looked like a man in drag.'

'Well of course he *would* say that,' she said. 'I've told you before, living with Josh is a terrible put-off.'

Shirley quite often begins her sentences with 'well of course', especially those relating to Josh. She has her own ideas about him and the reason we are friends. She is very fond of telling me that he likes me, of course, because I look like a boy. I did wonder this morning whether I was going to hear this again, but it was the red lipstick (one of her cast-offs) that had grabbed her attention. She said, 'You know, despite the fact that men – well, most of the men that I know – say they don't like too much, really they prefer plain girls who wear make-up to beautiful girls who don't, because *they* are making an effort. Men like us to make an effort you know, otherwise they say "I see you've let yourself go."'

I really hope that Shirley isn't right. Her version of life, love, women and men is one which makes me *want* to let myself go. Floating. Up into the air.

Oliver has come round today because Shirley and Andrew have gone off house hunting. They are hoping to move to the north of the city where Shirley assures me that the air is cleaner. I do worry that when they move I might never see him again. He's three. He's the only person I have known all his life. I don't like children, and I hope this isn't the reason I've made an exception in his case. He has soft brown hair and an enquiring look. His favourite thing to do when he comes round to our house is to make rose-petal perfume from one of Shirley's bushes that has spilled over our fence, and which Josh has trained to grow underneath his window.

Today he is sorting petals into piles according to size and shape. Each pile has twelve petals in because that's as far as he can count. He is possessed by an intensity of concentration that I have no recollection of in myself. Maybe one day. Sitting here watching him, I am aware, as I so often am with him, that these days we have together remain in his mind for only the shortest of spaces, soon to be collated into the murky swamp that is childhood. When he moves up north, if I never see him again, how long will he remember me? And I'll know him until I die.

I used to (and I still do sometimes, only now he doesn't take it seriously) try to take him back as far as he could go. When he began to speak I thought, it's not that long since he was in the womb, not that long before he was. And I'd sit him down and ask him questions, hoping he'd remember and I'd get an answer to the secret we're all longing to tell. Sadly nothing. And now he knows what I want to hear and makes up stories. Usually involving plots Andrew has read to him the night before. Before he was born he was a pirate, he was a wrestler and, most surprisingly, he was a small blue bicycle called Bertie.

Little scrap, he only weighed five pounds when he was born. I was fascinated to watch him and work out exactly when he acquired his edges. At first, he thought the whole wide world was the same person and that person was him. Admittedly he had his favourites, but if Shirley had died, or if I had died, he wouldn't have noticed. God needs us more than we need Him.

Oliver and I have discovered together that if you put rose petals into cold water and then boil them, the perfume is far more fragrant than if the water's warm to start with. Also the more water the better, but boiled off to just a tiny amount and then put in the blender to mush.

I have to say that the rose-petal perfume started as a demonic joke. A couple of years ago, Josh and I were convinced it was up to us to change everyone's opinion, especially Shirley's. We were unreasonably irritated by her 'being brought up without a father' conversations, which were usually followed by trite examples of her conjugal arrangements with Andrew. 'He and I just do the things we're best at,' she continues to explain, quite patiently, 'I do the girly things and he does the manly things, but that's because we're good at them.'

To Shirley, 'manly things' means taking out the rubbish.

In the days when Oliver only weighed five pounds and we would sometimes babysit, Josh used to lean over his cot and murmur 'Olivia! You're so pretty!' I doubt we'll ever know the outcome of that experiment. The perfume was another of his ideas but the joke was lost, to the great gain of all parties, because Oliver has never gone home smelling of roses and must never have mentioned to his mother how he's spent his afternoon. His secrecy is one of the qualities that has forced me to like him.

Today, Josh comes in just as we are decanting our brown musk into jam jars. He's carrying a bag of clothes from the local charity shops. He's got a red hat for me and a miniature skiing jacket for Oliver. They seem ridiculous in the heat of the summer and we laugh as we put them on. Oliver says, 'Can we jump now?' and we take an arm each and hurl him up into the air. We are custodians of his dizziness. We look at each other when we play this game and recognise our mutual jealousy. We wish we too could have two big people to make us feel weightless. We bought Oliver his baby-bouncer because we remembered what a sad day it was when we had to get out of ours. And the man who invented bungee jumping knows how we feel.

When Oliver leaves, I'll pour the results of our day on the garden. It would be more cyclical perhaps to feed them to the roots of the rosebush, but they're on the other side where I can't get to them. Plants eat their dead ancestors. I think this as I tip our perfume away. Plants are cannibals. More than this, they eat bits of their dead selves. Horrid.

Tonight, Josh and I have been invited to a party by a sort-of-friend of ours called Garry. The theme is Army Camp and everyone is to dress up in combat gear. We are goodtime girls, me and Josh, but we're not getting into fancy dress for anybody. I've persuaded him that we are totally within our rights to go in mufti.

Maybe 'goodtime girl' is a bit too optimistic. In a few hours' time I'll be persuading him not to go at all. I'm never sure whether I'm trying to talk him out of it or making him talk me into it. We always do go. We're always glad we've gone. It's like this, I've a friend who prefers women although she told me once she sometimes needs to sleep with men. In the morning she smiles and says to herself 'thank god I'm gay'. Parties and clubs and bars, they're always incredibly exciting in advance, and such a good idea afterwards. But while you're actually there? Somehow they make coming home such a relief.

As far as we can work out, at this one we'll know nobody there. Not as good as knowing everyone, but better than knowing a few people not very well and dreading they'll leave your side. Desperately trying to entertain them. Judging when you'll see their interest waning. Thinking on your toes of what to hit them with next.

Josh says this party won't be much of a talking one anyway, more a dancing. In that case it will depend entirely on the music. I wonder if we've steadily raised the volume over the past forty years to blot out our dwindling interest in chat. We used to clothe ourselves with words but now our armour is drugs and drums. It's easier behind these, requiring less, providing an excuse. What people say, what they do are no longer criteria by which to judge them. In the chaos of a rave, their behaviour, our reaction, cannot be trusted. We rely instead on being perspicacious. We get a 'good vibe' from this dancer here and 'the fear' from that other over there.

Still, it's fun isn't it? And it's not only the charity shops that Josh has been to. He pulls from his pocket his other purchases of this afternoon. Two microdots. I wink at him. Speed is scummy, coke is self-obsessed, E – I have spent evenings in my youth on E putting ice-cubes in the mouths of kissing couples, thinking they'd love it, maybe they did – I don't know, it's that enforced tribalism thing. I'd rather do it with people I really love, who I really think are beautiful. Acid is my favourite and he knows it.

It's not a great idea to take it before we've got ready before we've called a cab, but we're deciding to anyway. That way we'll have burnt our boats, that way we'll have to dress and go. Quickly and without thinking about it. And when we realise what we've done, we'll be there.

In the cab I know we're both checking the other for signs. I can see it in the way I'm looking at Josh, in the smile that's playing round his lips, we're both nearly giggling and I'm very aware of my cheeks. It's so exciting this waiting. It's a high in itself. What am I going to get? For once I know I'm going to get something. I'm definitely going to get something and I'm going to like it, but I don't know what it is yet. It's Christmas in heaven. All presents and no disappointments.

We find the street, we find the house. And I kind of don't want to go in because the something I'm going to get is not dependent on the party. I'd have a great time just tripping with Josh and far less frightening. I mean, what is this party going to achieve? Have I ever been to a party and made a new friend? I don't think so. No. Is this odd? Has anybody? The door is open but in front is a metal lattice which is locked and through which a girl is leaning. She has lost the plot, she's saying 'the philosophy is sound', I think. But she can't quite make her mouth move in conjunction with her voice so the effect is of some cheaply-dubbed film. From what I can make out behind her, she seems a valid example of the scene at large. Josh says, 'Will you get someone to let us in?' as though this is likely to happen. Please don't let it happen. From nowhere though Garry appears. He has an iron key on a chain. I look at Josh to tell him I'm still sober, I don't want to go in, hello! welcome to hell, but he smiles his in-for-a-penny smile and gives Garry a kiss. Garry locks the door behind us.

I can't get over the fact that Garry has locked the door. I mean, what if there's a fire? I want to point this out to Josh but somehow he's been swallowed by a mass of faces in the hall and Garry's leading me by the hand upstairs. I can't believe it. I'm going to lose Josh. It's my biggest fear and I'm having to confront it at the beginning of the evening. Without him, how will I get home? That whole taxi trauma, finding a number, making yourself heard, sitting off your head in the back and hoping they're normal – it's an ocean between me and my bed and Josh is the bridge. What happens if I don't find him again? I will find him – I'd ask Garry only, how ridiculous. I'm in a house. You can't lose a person in a house. Upstairs downstairs.

Upstairs seems a terribly long way. It must be like this for

Oliver. Always. Imagine having more stairs than numbers at your disposal. Like walking into the infinite. Like walking up a hill that apparently never ends. This is a hill. Too many people, like so many bushes and trees and boulders, blocking my view of the top. I can't see down, I can't see up, I squeeze Garry's hand to tell him to stop.

There's a sort of corner with a wider stair and room to rest. He's saying, 'Okay, sweetheart? Okay?' and rubbing my hand with his thumb. It feels delicious. Like the first time I've been touched. I'm nodding I think, I'm trying to smile. But that's just it: I've no idea if what's on the inside is getting through to the outside. He's saying 'Meet . . .' and then a sea of faces where our safe stair was. I can't meet, my mouth's all tremble. 'Meet Mary.' Mary. Mary. It sounds funny, Mary. I don't like her I think. Bad vibe. Oh definitely. She's pointing to something in her cleavage, she's saying 'Should I lose the Action Man?' She's only wearing a bra, a bra and a doll. Should it go, yes or no? She's demanding a decision. Don't stop rubbing my hand, Garry. My neck is too weak for my head. Baby me.

Up up up, we've got there, but where are we going? I say, 'Where are we going, Garry?' and he says, 'Yes'. Hopeless. More keys into a room, bed, cupboard, desk. Diet coke that he's giving me. I'm breathing. He's saying, 'Just relax. Just relax and go with it.' He smooths my eyebrows with his thumbs, he says, 'That's it. There's no one else in here.'

Will you kiss me, Garry. I know you don't, but will you? Would it be too horrid for you? A smile, and then a kiss and oh! it's dreamy. I feel like I'm sucking the life out of him, feel like he's feeding me. This is just what I wanted to earth me, now I'm slowing down.

Garry grins. He kisses my nose. He takes my hand and sits me on the bed. He takes off his top. I've never noticed before but he's got a beautiful body. Club culture. The gym. What would Henry VIII make of the gym? Lifting things that don't need to be moved. Running when nobody's chasing you. He's taken off his trousers, little cotton pants he's wearing, and now he's dressing in new clothes. Exactly the same but clean. He says, 'Ready?' and I say, 'Yes.'

Back downstairs – and there is Josh on the dining room dancefloor. He's surrounded by soldiers, giving it some where the table should be. He winks, he laughs, he takes my elbows and moves me to dance. I know how to do this. Find some space and start off small. Keep moving. Now feet, now arms, now hips perhaps. It's the call of the drums this music, pom pom pom. Pom pom pom and your body jerks to it – Don't look at anyone else yet cos they'll put you off your rhythm before you've found it and suck you into theirs. You might not be able to dance to theirs. Little jerks getting bigger until the music encapsulates you, and your body learns the beat. Then your mind can wander, then when the rhythm changes and the tune comes in it's like you're flying, endorphins rushing, your body a freeway of racing blood, you go like billyo and you're dancing, properly dancing, forgetting you're physical, forgetting you're dancing at all.

If we could float a little off the ground, would there be

any need for this? I see why whirling dervishes. I see why baby-bouncers. Roller coasters, swings, fast cars and dances. The end is this: after that rush to float, after that speed to take off.

There's Hideous Mary. Sans Ken. I don't like her trainers – perhaps that's why I don't like her. I turn round to ask Josh what he thinks but he's no longer there. Oh my god. No, he'll come back. Even if he doesn't I'll get home eventually. I won't be here this time tomorrow and that's what I must keep thinking. Thinking, thinking. It's so solitary, this. It's not socialising at all. And now I've remembered that I'm dancing. And now I'm going to have to start all over again. Looking like I'm having a good time. Until I am having a good time.

We've been here for four hours. Four hours ago I was snogging Garry in his bedroom. I can't believe I snogged Garry. Well yes, I can believe that – I can't believe Garry snogged me. Did Garry snog me? I was very high then, very high and now I'm not so – so in four hours' time I'll be pretty much back to normal. Hooray for normality. Hooray for coming home. When Josh comes back I'll brave going to the loo. It's a terrifying prospect I know, but think this: you're in a house. If it were daylight you wouldn't give it a second thought. There'll be people and you might trip up, but that's the very worst. And Josh must be there now so Josh can tell you where it is and maybe, if he's feeling kind, Josh will come with you.

Fingers and buttons, they're the tricky bit – it makes Josh laugh that it takes me so long. I say, 'Cut me some slack,' which makes him laugh more because it sounds so peculiar. I laugh too. Hysteria on the bathroom floor. No, no, I've got to stop this, I've got to go to the loo. Concentrate. Buttons push through buttonholes. These things I've learnt go first. Zips and trousers under my fingers, the space from me to the lavatory, but my instincts are intact. Inside, my body carries on without me. I am a machine, a clockwork toy, and I'll go until the last turn of the key.

Josh tells me that he's found the chill-out room, and this is where we're headed. Inside, a mound of cushions, a sofa and an armchair. Hideous Mary is collapsed on the cushions, Josh has colonised the armchair, leaving me with space for one buttock beside three men on the sofa. They look like triplets. Shaved heads, combat trousers and tight white tee shirts. They're having a conversation about some girl. In front, two dancers moving like the wind. One's saying 'This is my favourite bit coming up.'

'The elephant bit?'

'Elephant?'

'Yes, listen,' and he's making a childish trunk and doing an impression. There are elephants in this world, it suddenly occurs to me. Right now, there are elephants. Doing their own thing.

One of the clones beside me has had enough. He says definitively, 'Look, she won't age well.'

'What are you on? Those cheekbones!' I turn to look at them and hear, 'See what I mean?' and realise with some horror that they're talking about me. It's one against two in praise of my longevity. I can't handle this now. I'm not at my best. My face feels like one of Picasso's. I close my eyes and hope they'll go away. They don't. I deal with it. I congratulate myself for not freaking out. I open my eyes and Josh says, 'You are such a wreck,' and laughs. This is not great for a girl's confidence. Thank god it's getting light and we could conceivably go home. I say 'Shall we go home?' and astoundingly, he says 'Yes'.

We decide to walk for twenty minutes and then catch the first train. Our ears are ringing still with the sounds of our night – techno track on auto-reverse, early-morning birdsong mixed in with the beat. Josh looks flushed, his skin thin, I think I see his blood vessels moving behind it. But he is normal compared to the weirdos on the train. Whenever I've travelled at this time there have only been strangers. And I've never been certain if it's me or it's them. I keep my eyes on Josh. Safe. I hold his hand on the escalator. Behind I am faintly aware of someone running, then someone tapping me, me? then someone putting a bit of paper in my hand and catching the stairs back down. Josh and I are in shock. He says, 'What does it say?'

'"Colin" and a phone number.' It's not just me, is it? It is an odd thing to do.

Josh shrugs – later – and threads my hand through his arm. Later we'll pick through the events of the evening, later decide we've had a brilliant time. But sleep first. Sleep. The sun is rising. Herald of a beautiful day we're going to miss.

And Shirley and Oliver are just waking up.

three

August is the room of a party an hour before dawn. What was last night sparkly and exciting has now begun to fall apart and stink a little. It's unpleasant and you want to leave but you can't quite. Because on the other side of it, there's only Today.

Is hot air thinner than cold air? And if so, what's missing? I could find out the answers to both these questions but (it's a freedom I take so much for granted that) I won't bother to. I do imagine though, living before anyone knew and no one could tell. The air is very thin this August and it's confusing me. It's as if the last few months of evaporating bodies, steaming dogshits, hot-baked rubbish and car exhausts are having their effect now. Strangely though, the air seems thinner. There's nothing in it to breathe. I hate August. And beyond it, only winter.

Nothing to take my mind off it but Colin. The most unlikely stories are the sweetest ones. We haven't got over it yet, we keep saying, 'Wow' and 'I can't believe I've found you' and 'Just say I hadn't felt brave'. We have been lovers for six months now and have slipped into an easy intimacy. It amazes me (but only in retrospect) how reality shifts and is just accepted. I no longer hesitate before I say the words 'my boyfriend'. Now when I go to Edward's house, I don't sleep in Lily's Room, but with Colin – in the best pink spare on the second floor.

Of course, I took my life in my own hands when I went off to meet him – it's something we fondly laugh about now. When I rang him he said 'I didn't think you'd call,' and I said, 'Neither did I.' Surely though, such a spontaneous gesture deserved a return. More than this I was flattered and it had to go somewhere. It wouldn't be much of a story would it? if 'And what happened then?' was followed by 'Nothing'. Memories are things you have to earn. Besides, I wasn't playing *that* high-risk a strategy, rapists and murderers are not the majority. I met him in a public place on a Saturday afternoon. What did we talk about? I can't remember now – everything. No. Nothing I'd ever talked about before. And Josh likes him.

The underground's a strange setting for a love scene and not one that I would have chosen. Tonight I'm on it to go to meet Edward. It's so hot that I've not bothered to fight for a seat but am standing by the window to the carriage next door. It's open for ventilation but it always makes me laugh, the thought of ventilation down here. If I stand the right way round my hair is in my eyes and up my nose, so I'm standing the wrong way round with it blowing off my face and I'm looking into the neighbouring car. Another set of possibilities in there. Perhaps it would have made all

the difference if I'd been on that side and looking in here
– if I'd been just five feet further down that day, Colin
would never have seen me – so do things happen because
they're supposed to? or just because they can? Chances are,
it's possible.

Edward and I are going for a walk after work in the
park. In the winter these are reserved for Sunday after-
noons, when he doesn't seem to notice that it's raining
and freezing cold. On the way back we get stuck in the
week-again traffic. He says, 'C'mon c'mon c'mon; c'mon
c'mon c'mon; *c'mon c'mon c'mon*' over and over under his
breath like a mantra. At his flat we sit in front of his
lookalike fire and drink tea (if I can be bothered to make
it). He cleans his shoes on the Sunday magazines and makes
me read to him from their papers. He lends me a dry pair
of socks (which I never return) and I catch the train home.
Sometimes he walks me to the station.

The park is a long way by underground, until it becomes
overground and almost until the end of the line. Tonight
though I suppose I'm enjoying it. It's quite nice, this breeze
on my face and those people to watch and this film in my
head where I've spent the next six months in love with
Colin. And it's so bizarre down here. It's science fiction.
Shunting through tunnels under the earth and in the dark
(it's always dark in science fiction). It reminds me of those
pictures for children where the earth's sliced through: *here
are the people walking the streets and here are the people
travelling beneath*. So many people, like bunnies in burrows,
like patients on their way to some spooky experiment in

a secret laboratory. And not one of them taking any notice of me. If I made such an impression on Colin why not so on them?

I'm making a mental note not to talk to Edward about Colin – he is a purist when it comes to conversations. The problem with mine, according to him, is their tendency to be experience-led. He doesn't like to know what I've 'been up to', he's not the least bit interested in plot – if I try to tell him he'll say, 'This isn't a conversation, Lily, it's a soliloquy.' So to get his views on the subject I'll have to couch it in altogether different terms. I'll have to conceptualise. Colin will have to become a debate about – I don't know quite what yet. I've got three more stops to work it out.

Edward and I have been coming to this park ever since we met. It's a pastime which belongs to him though and not to me. I'm sure he brings other people on similar trips while I'd never dream of coming with other than him. It's his place. He's never said so, though. It's his possession and he has no need to point it out. When we first became friends we'd fill our pockets with bottles of beer and walk up the hill to see the sun set. We'd sit and watch it getting drunk on its glory, mostly in silence but pointing out the occasional flash of colour till it had ended. Then, humbled, Edward would give his views on how he'd have improved it.

There he is waiting for me in the front of his car. He's in his usual position, feet on the steering wheel, bum in midair, swapping his suit for something more suited to walking. No attempt at discretion. I can tell by the way he's yanking on his jeans that he's not in good temper. Well, he never is for the first five minutes, like he finds it hard to make the change from his own good company to someone else. He glares at my feet as I get in beside him, I say, 'I've got my trainers in my bag.'

'We're going for a stomp, Lily, do you know what that means? It means working your lazy blood around your lazy body, working up a sweat, moving fast and covering a lot of distance and if there's even the smallest chance that you're going to make me cut it short because your feet hurt, then you'd better get out now.'

'You always lay this on me, and I've never complained my feet hurt.'

'Well, you must have done once, or else I wouldn't say it. So what's it to be?'

'I'll be fine.'

'Good,' he says, and he speeds off.

Edward has always driven like a maniac. He says he does it to calm himself down. I remember the first time he took me to his parents' house he swerved down the tiny country lanes as though he were the only person likely to be using them. He turned to me at ninety miles-an-hour and said, 'At least if we die we'll die together,' which I didn't find exactly relaxing. But then, I'm not friends with Edward that I might relax. I'm friends with him for lots of other reasons which I've suddenly completely forgotten. I'm not in the mood to deal with his mood, I'm fighting one of my own. Beyond this light summer evening, beyond this lovely walk, beyond this beautiful park and the friend that I love, it's August, and winter ahead.

I surrender. Edward always does this and I always put up with it; I've stood on a sweating train for an hour to get here and at least he could be slightly pleased to see me; if I did to him what he constantly does to me our friendship would be over in five minutes; and whereabouts along the line did we agree that he was allowed to be a crotchety old git and I patient till he'd got over it? I feel like making a big gesture, I feel like telling him to stop the car and getting out without explanation, I feel like going home and never seeing him again. But I can't, I won't, I don't, and this makes me crosser. My throat starts to throb and tears fill the backs of my eyes. I sometimes think it's this pain in my neck and not the pain from anything else which makes me start crying – it's unbearable and tears the only way to clear it. I can't cry though, I can't cry with Edward here in the front with me – nothing's happened. Nothing unusual. This is the way he always is for the first five minutes, and nothing's happened today to warrant this bad temper. Nothing unusual. But it's like this mood is always lurking, like it's easy to give into, like once I've crossed the line it's such a job to send away.

We park the car in our usual place with the hill out in front of us. It's seven o'clock and the summer light has brought out the punters. They play with their dogs, they play with their children, they even play with balls (I've never understood the attraction), they lie on their backs and they look at the sky with their fingers knotted in the

hair of the one they love. Little boys fly kites and float
model boats on the water. Why is this fun? I'd rather be
the kite, I'd rather be the boat. 'My God,' I say 'there's
even someone doing Yoga.'

'There's a hint of scorn in your voice.'

'No there isn't.'

'There is – scorn and envy.'

'I'm not envious.'

'Are you in sparring mode this evening?' he says, joking,
but I take it badly, 'Because if you are I don't need to
remind you who always wins.'

I hate Edward. I hate him tonight. He's smug and we
always do what he wants to do. We'll begin our walk as
usual in the Louisa Plantation and then he'll make me
march up that hill – which is agony but I never complain
– and we won't be allowed to stop at the top to look at
the view but we'll have to run down the other side, and then
continue for another half an hour at least before returning
to his car, where he'll put my life in danger all the way
back to his flat, where he'll neglect to offer me tea.

I love Edward though, I'll love him always, and how else
would I have any of our walks, which are usually perfect?
how else would I have him? I'm not really cross about any
of these things – so what is it that I'm cross about? Somewhere I'm laughing at myself sulking but what makes me
sulk more is that I just wish one part of me would win,
would be it, would be me.

No one remembers who Louisa was, but her garden is
a tropical paradise of waxy leaves and stupidly beautiful

33

flowers, and you can't hear the traffic from here. As we go in Edward says, 'It's all just going over. We should have come two weeks ago. Never mind.'

'Never mind?'

'I rather like it like this. Everything fermenting on its stalk.'

'I'd have preferred it spectacular and two weeks ago.'

'But there's something so decadent – don't you think? – about it, and I like the smell.'

'Of rotting flowers?'

'Perhaps I was a maggot in a former life,' and then, 'What's that?'

'I'm not playing.'

'Only cos you don't know.'

'I do know.'

'What is it then?'

'An iris.'

'No, it's a gladioli. Come on, we're going to our bench.'

I wonder with how many others of his friends Edward refers to this as 'our bench'. I'm trying not to. Admittedly not that hard. It looks onto a pond from which you get a double dose of colour – first on the bank, then reflected in the water. He sits down. He never sits up straight. He says, 'You're right, it would have been spectacular two weeks ago.'

I say, 'A garden takes such a lot of work and it's all over so quickly. Bud bloom rot, it slightly freaks me out.'

'Yes. But then it starts all over again.'

'I know. It's a wonder nature doesn't get bored.'

'Like you, you mean?'

I say, 'I spent all last winter looking forward to summer, and now it's August, and I'm going to spend all next winter doing the same.'

'Well I'm sure you're going to be doing other things as well. Let's not get too dramatic.'

'You know how when you're a child, time seems to go really slowly? I've always wondered why that is. I mean, surely time should go more quickly then, when everything's new and exciting, and slowly now when everything's predictable and the same.'

'I said that to you.'

'No you didn't.'

'I said that to you the last time I was bored.'

'Well, you should be flattered that I think it's worth repeating.'

'Yes – and here's something else for you that's worth repeating: Boredom is one thing that time doesn't heal. You can get bored of being miserable or bored of longing for something that you can't have, but you can't get bored of being bored.'

'So?'

'So spur yourself into action. Make some effort, Lily. Do something.'

'Like what? Anything I *do* will only be a temporary measure. Everything's a temporary measure and that's what's depressing.'

'Well, get used to it,' he says, 'You're in for the duration.'

* * *

No doubt I've missed the point he's making, but our conversation has made up my mind. I get home, I find the piece of paper and I do it immediately. When I tell him who I am Colin says, 'I didn't think you'd call.'

I say, 'Neither did I.'

'I don't blame you,' he says, 'you must have thought I was a nutter.'

'You still could be,' I say.

He says, 'The thing is, I was in the same carriage as you a few days before. I never thought I'd see you again – and when I did . . .'

'How bizarre,' I say.

'Yes,' he laughs, 'how bizarre.'

It's always a little unnerving when someone's shared a moment with you of which you're unaware. Once from the top deck of a bus stuck in traffic I saw Josh ambling along the pavement. He'd become one of a multitude of strangers making their way to various destinations, and, not aware that he was being watched, was showing himself to me so carelessly, so entirely, it felt rude to be observing – but I couldn't look away. I've never told him. You always fancy yourself invisible, don't you? going about your business, thinking your own thoughts, but Colin watched me in the carriage. And this is why it's startling: here I'm the narrator, there I'm just the extra, entering and exiting stage right, stage left but suddenly we're meeting: Centre Stage.

At this time of the year there's a fairground set up in the middle of town. A merry-go-round made of horses (they're boring), a big wheel, a roller coaster, waltzers, slot machines, ducks to shoot, toys to win and massive sticks of miraculous candyfloss. This is the place Colin has chosen for our first date. Ten out of ten for originality. The thing that's worrying me is I can't remember what he looks like, I'm not sure I ever knew. I've arranged to meet him by the 2p jackpots, but I'd quite like to know which one he is before he knows it's me so I've got the choice to slip away . . . It's quite exciting though. I'm taking my phone in case of emergency and Josh is to call it every two hours to check on me. He's slightly excited too. We've laughed, he's said, 'You're going under cover.'

There are several clusters of 2p jackpots, each arranged to a hexagonal beehive effect. Standing at one booth gives a through-view of the others, their hydraulic shelves ebbing and flowing, pushing mounds of coins hardly, but tantalisingly, nearer the edge where they *could* fall down the chute and into my pocket. The only person at this one is a thirteen-year-old boy with a perfect sense of timing. He watches the players at all the machines and just as their change has run out takes over their game and scoops in their cash. There's an irritating jingle playing over and over, the theme to some Sunday sports programme, which this boy is using (it looks like) to work out exactly when to drop his coin. At every booth a different beat. He taps his foot. He concentrates. His breath shows on the glass in front of him and he goes for it – it's incredible, he wins every time. I notice I'm grinning. There's something so satisfying in the sound, all that money clanking down.

'Who wants a handful of 2ps?' someone says to me, bursting my cloud. 'I don't understand the attraction, do you?'

I hope this isn't Colin.

'Lily,' he says, 'are you early or am I late?'

Colin is quite good-looking. He has dark hair and dark eyes. His hair has grown out of the style it had six months ago and it flops in different partings which he rearranges with a flick of his hands, a nervous twitch. His hands are bony but he bites his nails. He's scruffy but it's not by accident. On the Big Wheel I notice that the brown centre in one of his eyes has seeped a little into its white, a trickle of colour that's blurring its edge. I wonder if he sees the same? It's like he's cried so much he's made it run. He's smiling and I realise I'm staring – I didn't mean it like *that*, but I don't say anything. 'Can you see where you live?' I ask, and I look at the view.

It's awkward to begin with, but the fairground's an excellent place for a first date. The rides provide a change of scene every five minutes, taking the pressure off what to say next. You'd have thought it would be easier, wouldn't you? with a total stranger not to run out of conversation – all their stories you haven't yet heard, all yours your friends have grown tired of. Not so though, not so and I wonder why this is. Too much choice perhaps, too little information. Everything I did last week means nothing if he doesn't know the players, and there's no such thing as news with someone new.

Here, though, we're having an adventure and we're having it together. Inside this freeze-framed 'now' we know each other well already. We've got to teasing stage, we're saying, 'I'll come with you on the Wall but not if you're going to scream.'

'I don't scream!'

'Like you didn't on the roller coaster? Don't think I didn't notice.'

'Chicken shit.'

'Yeah you are.' We're having fun us two together. Colin likes Lily. Lily likes him.

On the carousel he tells me about his family. He's got three younger brothers much littler, the eldest's seventeen, the youngest one's five. For special treats the youngest rings him up and it's a great event when the eldest comes to stay. And what about the middle? 'He's kind of strange,' says Colin. 'There's this girl back home who fancies him and Mum and Dad keep teasing him about her, and the last time I rang I said, "Why don't you, you know, go for it?" and d'you know what he said?'

'No.'

'He said, "She's got really horrible hands."' I laugh. I think, 'It's amazing the brain'. If our two lives merge from this moment I'll store his 'pre-me' stories, if not, bury them, sometime to recall at random: *Who was it who ate nuts on toast? Ah yes, that Colin person, that train encounter, that strange afternoon at the fair.*

Do you think people like fair rides because they make you go *I'm going to die, I'm going to die . . . I'm alive!* ? I'd ask Colin but we're spinning so fast on the waltzer my mouth won't work. I'm trying to stay on my side and he's trying to stay on his side – so hard that when our bodies crash, it hurts. We give in. We meet in the middle, jumble up and it's painless, his arms round my shoulders, my hands on his knees. When the ride ends though we're bashful, we're briefly embarrassed, we're ashamed by our – accidental – physical contact. The only cure is some more but on purpose. I kiss him, I make it the norm, and it's okay.

four

Once upon a time, a long long time ago, was there somebody in the world who knew more than anybody else in the world? who had read every single book that had ever been written? who knew all there was to know about science, mathematics, theology, philosophy, literature and art? and if so, was he the cleverest man alive?

A long long time ago, just at that point before there were too many equations, laws, credos, doctrines to be swallowed by a single mind, it would have been possible for one person's consciousness to be greater than the sum of everybody else's. Never before would there have been a man so well-informed as he; proportionately, never would there be again. But he wasn't the cleverest man alive, just the holder of all available information. Knowledge does not equal intelligence, stupidity has little to do with ignorance – it's not thick I'm feeling, no, it's in the dark. See, I'm not sure where to go from here. This story has been rolling along in the present tense, for in the present one is always right. Colin, though, Colin will be in the past.

How right can a person ever be? Only as right as the amount of information that they've got, and unless they're God there's always more. We were absolutely right when we thought the earth was flat, we found out we were wrong and now we're absolutely right again. There's no such thing as progression. The more we know, not the more right we become. We were wrong in the past, we are right in the present, and in the future? Todays become yesterdays, tomorrows become today.

Yesterday, Colin invited me to dinner. And you know how it is sometimes when you kiss a person and then you want to see them again? It isn't always because you like them. You think it is, but really it's because you're wondering why you did it, and if you'll be tempted again; it's because one kiss alone seems something like a waste; it's because although you're always meeting people and finding them this way or that way, you don't care much how they've found you unless you've kissed them, but somehow if you've kissed them, they hold your definition.

Colin didn't call me for two weeks after I'd kissed him, and for those two weeks I was not worth knowing. If I was pretty, it was only from afar; if I was interesting, it didn't extend beyond an afternoon; if I was funny, not funny enough; if I was kind, so what? None of these things merited more than just one kiss from Colin.

Have you ever been plagued by if-only-I-hadn'ts and maybes? For hours longer than they had actually lasted, I went over and over the events of our afternoon. I replayed them a hundred different ways which may have been preferable, I steered myself at imagined junctions and took a left or took a right, I paused myself at the moment I kissed him – it's a temporary madness and one which has afflicted me before – and I wished that I'd never kissed Colin. A comment of his kept coming back to me, waking me up as I was falling asleep on weeknights, keeping me conscious on Saturday mornings trying to doze. It was this, something he said just after I'd kissed him; he said, 'I wasn't going to do that today.' No, he said, 'I promised myself I wasn't going to do that today.' Today. Surely then, he was expecting some tomorrow? At the point where he promised himself today, he imagined a tomorrow. Did I blow tomorrow? Did I blow tomorrow by kissing him today? Or did I just blow tomorrow? Just by being me? For if everything that Shirley says is true then I should have played the game, but I don't think I am able to. That whole courtship ritual she goes on about like the birds and the bees do – you see it on nature programmes, you see it in the pigeons in the park – hes chase, shes run away; that whole fighting chasing winning thing, 'it's natural', it just don't come natural to me. I don't do hunter and hunted, I don't do chaser and chaste, I don't do nurturing or nesting or breast-feeding – but if everything that Shirley ever says is true I'll have to don't-do all these things alone, won't I? Colin. Won't I do?

This was how I was thinking, for most of every hour, most of every hour of every day for two whole weeks. About Colin, I imagined, although now I realise that it wasn't at all. (I wonder for how many weeks more I could have gone on thinking, if he hadn't called me? I could have called him, but I pretend I'm old-fashioned in this respect.)

This was how I was thinking, anxiously replaying the minutiae of an afternoon, worrying about the bigger questions these raised about my personality, thinking about a future (what kind of future?) and then, No one around me is aware. Josh and I pretend we couldn't care less about the people we meet, not wanting to let on that our teenage arrogance has given way to something more delicate, that our surety that we are Special hangs by a gossamer thread. So I didn't tell Josh; of course I didn't tell Edward; I didn't tell Shirley or the girls in my office because it's a lesson I learnt very early on. It'd be lovely if you could say 'Yeah, I kissed this person,' or, 'Yeah, I slept with that person, and I like him, and I hope it happens again,' but no matter how much your friends think of you, you've always been slightly got the better of when a romance ends before it's begun. I got up in the mornings, went to work, came home, ate, went to bed, and none of my colleagues or cronies was ever aware (I am alone).

Anyway, he did call, and magically everything was restored. He offered no excuse for his two week silence and, of course, I didn't ask for any. He wondered if I'd like to go to the movies? I said I'd love to. We talked awkwardly until such time had elapsed as was decent and then we arranged to meet, five days later, in the foyer.

He was not yet there when I arrived – no matter how hard I try I always turn up on time. I was in a state of some excitement. In the intervening days since our non-event of a conversation I'd had several, more fruitful chats with him – in the bath or walking along the pavement, in the nighted reflection of myself in French windows (smoking a cigarette). I'd laughed, I'd told him of past loves, I'd mentioned all those stupid things that worry me, I'd pretended he was on spare chairs at tables next to Edward, next to Shirley, next to Josh and I'd played to his gallery; I'd put him in my bed and whispered my friendships and their political history; I'd told him all the stories of possession littered round my room – I'd had a wonderful imaginary time with him, and now, here he would be for real.

I rarely enjoy a film, but I love going to the cinema – the way the decor hasn't changed since the 1950s, the way the carpet extends halfway up the wall and decorates the chairs, the space-age swirls on the ceiling, the bizarre lighting fixtures and the too-grand curtain; I love that lingering smell of popcorn (sweet like urine); those unsophisticated adverts that warn you about bag thieves and ask you not to smoke, that sell orange squash and frankfurters and a curry from the Indian next door; I love the way that outside it may be day or night, winter or summer, but in here it is always twilight, always a little too warm. I like to sit in the front row and stretch my legs out. I like to sit down and *then* take my coat off so I'm that bit more cocooned. I like to place my things around me, bag, sweets, drink, and settle into (for the next two hours) my home.

I spotted Colin as soon as he walked in. He was trying to look cool but he was looking for me. I watched him.

He caught my eye and came over. He said 'Hi,' and gave me a kiss on the cheek. Just the one. I noticed he'd shaved. I noticed he smelt a little too strongly of not-all-that-pleasant eau de cologne (lemon?), but I let it go. Women find that kind of thing endearing. We bought our tickets and we took our seats, not in the front row but in the middle, in the middle of the middle. Not that I minded.

I didn't mind anything that evening. The film was one of those slick thrillers with every shot a photographic masterpiece, with the hero's dark side just light enough for us to care, with his subplot home life prodding the heart with the glory of the human spirit, and with every plot point throwing up questions left unanswered till the final minute, so we'd all feel stupid, stupid, missing the point and then, Supremely Clever as the credits rolled. It was a good film, and not one I'd ever choose to go and see. Afterwards, he asked what I'd like to do next and I suggested going for a curry in the advertised restaurant. I'm not sure if he knew I was joking. It was full, so we wandered about for a bit wondering what to do, and then he said, if I'd like it, he'd make me pasta at his place. We hadn't really hit it off. Up to this point, we hadn't really – but then, there wasn't much of a chance to chat during the movie, and he'd been nervous afterwards when we found ourselves with Nothing Planned, and I suppose that after the rapport we'd struck up in the five days of my imagination, reality was faced with something of a challenge.

Once or twice in the past I've been out for the evening

with a man and I've not enjoyed it terribly but still I've gone home with him afterwards, and it's kind of in the hope that once we are there, or once we are there and under the comfort of a duvet, we'll start to get on. So I said yes to Colin's pasta invitation. I hate pasta, but I said yes.

It was a sweet flat. The kitchen felt kitsch, its wallpaper out of some 1940s nursery, the cupboards painted pastel blue. The bathroom had a freestanding bath and a tier of hanging baskets filled with bric-a-brac – soaps, old candles and spider plants – unusual and pleasing, I thought, for a boy. There were two bedrooms (he said he had a lodger called Jacques) but no sitting room; there were fireplaces, but no central heating; he'd ripped up the carpets, but he hadn't got around to polishing the floor. From underneath one of its boards he produced a bottle of wine (he told me he kept it there so that Jacques wouldn't find it), he poured me a glass and he cooked.

The meal was absolutely disgusting, and not just because I hate pasta. He burnt the garlic bread, he put no salt in the bolognese sauce and the spaghetti was overdone. I felt sorry for him, but no, I didn't really feel, I was sorry in a supremely detached way as though I'd never left the cinema. I found myself observing him – his nerves, his flicking the hair from his face as he had at the fair, his wondering what to say next, his get-out clause which was showing me through his photo album (all his family there, just as he'd described), his telling me that he could play the spoons and giving me a demonstration – all of this produced in me no feeling at all, not even the vaguest sense of curiosity.

It had just turned September and although there was no real chill in the air, I suggested we light a fire. We sat in front of it, kissing a bit. I remembered with some alarm those two weeks before his phone call – weeks of madness, weeks during which I'd made him custodian of my personality and I realised that I'd spent so much time wondering what Colin thought about me that I'd completely forgotten to wonder what I thought about him. What did I think about him? Why, nothing. Why nothing? He asked me if I'd stay the night. I said yes.

I remember once I had a boyfriend. Not for very long, but the brevity of our affair was indirectly proportional to the largeness of my feeling for him. Once I got up from being in bed with him to go to the bathroom, but sleepy and unused to the layout of his rooms I wandered into his cupboard by mistake. It was large, quite large enough to walk into and turn around, and I found myself surrounded by all his clothes, hangers full of shirts, velvet trousers, jeans, old dressing gowns, shoes and shoe boxes. I wanted to spend an age in that cupboard that smelt of him, that seemed a secret I'd discovered, learning by heart its contents, their history; but he called out to me, I remember, he called out, 'What are you doing in there? Come back to bed,' and I never had occasion to step inside again.

Why the difference between that man and this? Colin's clothes were hanging on a rail beside his bed, there was a desk in front of the window with a few magazines on it and a computer, and the mantelpiece above the fireplace held photographs and postcards – some turned the writing-way-round. I read them out of politeness. I noticed a fax on the desk from his father, wishing him a happy birthday ('you old fart'), but I didn't wonder if he were a Taurus or a Gemini; I wondered why his bric-a-brac bathroom, his excellent taste in wine and his ability to play an unusual musical instrument were not enough for me to find him interesting. Not that he was boring. Objectively, there was nothing about him (and nothing going on in my life) that should stop me wanting to become trapped in his closet, but I didn't want to be trapped. And would I ever? I doubted it. Factor X was missing.

We took off our clothes matter-of-factly. I wondered if he'd keep his pants on. He didn't. He said sweetly, 'I've got a duck-down duvet,' and we got underneath it. It was very warm inside. Too warm – it made my mental discomfort physical. He tried to touch me but I put my arms around him. I said, 'I don't want to have sex tonight,' ('Tonight') and I smiled a twisted smile at myself. We hugged for a while, we whispered nonsense to each other until he fell asleep and then I turned around and fell asleep too.

He woke up while I was still dozing. He tossed and turned and tried to settle down, he tried to be as peaceful as I was but it didn't work, and soon his restlessness made it impossible for me to stay sleeping. I was glad he was awake first. It was in line with something I've been noticing for a little while which is, when I'm the first one to wake (usually hours too early), when I try to get comfy again and talk myself into falling back to sleep, when I wonder whether to put my arm around the person lying next to me it's a certain sign that Factor X is very definitely present, and I was glad – not that it wasn't, but that my sleeping was in keeping with this. I opened my eyes and Colin smiled at me. I said to myself, That's another thing that happens when you're the first one to wake: you long for the day to begin so the two of you can be together again, but all that actually happens is that the day does begin, and you get up, and say goodbye.

When we said goodbye I gave him a kiss on the lips. It had been awkward and hurried until then, but I gave him a kiss on the lips – a couple of kisses – and for a moment it was cosy. We were comfortable kissing each other. I didn't say 'I'll ring you', because it annoys me when people say that if it means that they won't; I said, 'Thank you for supper.'

He said, 'Your turn next time.'

'I'm a terrible cook,' I said and I left. It was my only lie.

Once I'd turned the corner of his road I realised I didn't really know where I was or how to get home. I walked down the street, hoping for a bus stop, feeling self-conscious in last night's clothes, especially in last night's footwear, which didn't seem at all relevant this bright Sunday morning. I wished I were Josh. Josh would look up at the sun or something and say 'Ah yes, we need to go left', so I called him on my mobile to ask his advice. He looked me up on his street map. He said, 'You're about fifteen minutes' walk away,' and decided to talk me through it. It was fun. He gave a direction and while I was following it, interrogated me about the night before. I was saying, 'Well, we got back to his flat and – right I'm at the zebra crossing, where do I go from here?' It was like a treasure hunt, the certain prize being home, it lifted my spirits because I was feeling a bit downcast, a little bit nasty, a little bit sullied – you know how it is? You have some sort of sexual encounter and you feel a bit traumatised, you've a little bit lost your reality, forgotten yourself, played the part you've always played in this plot, in this set, with a hundred different casts before. You need to remember who you are on a daily basis – what you find funny, who loves you, what they all think of you, they who don't know you in this context, stroking a stranger's head. Anyway, Josh talked me through it until I got to my front door, and once I'd got to my front door, last night had become just another funny story, just another strange encounter in a city full of strange encounters, full of lives crashing into each other and rebounding, bouncing back home.

five

Poor Colin, he showed me his home – I think that's the worst of it. For as much as that boy with the cupboard shattered my heart, he never saw where I lived and that was some comfort. If he had, where would I have run to? If he had, each room would have tasted unclean; my decor, my possessions (all carefully chosen) he would have rejected; and he could have imagined me – ruined – inside of the walls of my home. As it was, he'd never be able to picture me there, so there I found solace. I was safe (somewhat safer, at least) in a place I could still call my own.

No such succour for Colin, who's been ringing me daily – his first call came within hours of Josh talking me home. It is strange, but no matter how good an actor (or actress) your previous night's partner, there's an automatic warning bell sounds off when you won't be lying in the dark with them again. Then comes that urge to make contact merely minutes after final contact has been made. I hate that urge, I rarely give in to it – it never assuages anything, never counts for your side. Still, Colin succumbed and reached for the receiver, and I hate to admit this (well, perhaps it's not true) but I bet if he'd waited his usual two weeks before seeming to remember, I'd have longed for his call, and longed for, I bet, the occasion to make a less delible impression.

But. There is nothing to long for. Except, perhaps, for Colin to leave me alone. Some people, though, insist on persisting, and this behaviour is so alien to my own that I cannot forgive him. In his absence, I have started to hate him. Finally, after two weeks of daily phone calls (but always during office hours when he knew I'd not be there) I rang him back and arranged to meet him – partly because I felt rather mean, partly because Josh kept looking at me accusingly, and partly because I couldn't bear for there to be any more messages on my machine. The past five days have been answer-phone free and been heaven (but perhaps the hell of tormenting another is worse than being tormented oneself?) but tonight I've to meet him – for a 'quick bite to eat' after work . . .

Do you ever look ahead to all the things you've got to pass beyond, this week or next week, and think to yourself 'after that I'll be straight'? or 'after that I'll be up to date'? 'after that my life will begin'? My real life. But *after that* never comes. *That* draws nearer to become *this*, a hideous hermaphrodite, hatching horribly in its belly a whole series of *this-and-thats*, cause giving birth to effect, effect growing up to become cause. I keep waiting for my life to begin. I keep waiting for that defining moment which will explain to me everything that's gone before, everything that is to come. Nothing though, just episodes. Just this. Just that.

Remember how it is? Sometimes. Rarely. When the prospect of *this evening* makes you smile at shopkeepers, makes you walk around all day like a prophet with a vision. Zen? I understand. Everything Is – exactly as it's meant to be. And when this evening comes (eventually), I'll find that I believe in someone else so utterly I'll feel I must have made them up. It's like a mist is lifted, all other lives were wrong but this is right; God *must* exist, miracles must happen, this must be Meant To Be and I must be eternal (or have a soul in any case, for now it's found its mate); no more dismal Sunday evenings, no more boring New Year's Eves, no more worries of returning after parties. Everything Is, a question, and its answer is, yes please.

So, no thanks, Colin. Thanks, but no. For even if it's true that zen is just a glimpse that comes, then goes away, that glimpse is still integral. So what's the point of seeing you?

If meeting you tonight would promise *that was that*, perhaps. But that does not exist, That means This.

Mid-afternoon at work I shut my door, find the piece of paper on which you have written COLIN and your phone number, and dial it up. It's a couple of beats before I press that final digit, but I'll only get your answer-machine (like you got mine). My message says 'I don't want to meet you tonight' – is it final enough? Surely.

And then it's the end of the day, like any other. Like any other I walk down the road that leads to the train taking me home. I should feel relieved, but I don't.

I run a bath, unclothe myself, step in. That same body that Colin touched, same foot, calf, knee being lowered into steaming water. Same thigh, never much attractive; same hip, buttock, ribcage, less so after Colin's eye. Neck, arms, head – rather insubstantial, aren't I? This bath could be my death bed; this, all the space that I require, all the room I occupy. I bury my head beneath the water; beneath the water I feel my hands along my body, that boundary between You and I. Which bit is most like me, I wonder, and whereabouts on it am I? Perhaps I'll always be my own lover – a Lily within a Lily; and without: edges.

Lying on my bed, boiling hot from my bath, my head trying to make a puddle in the pillow, I think again, 'Perhaps I'll always be my own lover'. My edge is where I'm at, most apparent in the things in my room, things I've been collecting over the years; things which didn't imagine themselves next to the things in Colin's room; things which looked at those things in Colin's room indifferently, which saw nothing worth looking at again; *my* things, which seemed so intriguing to me when I was intrigued by Colin, when I led him on that imaginary tour through my life (*but perhaps I'll always be my own lover*) before seeing him for real at the cinema; those things seem rather silly now he really won't be seeing them – silly, ridiculous, evidence of an all-too-common personality: eccentric, belonging only to itself; seeing only through the chink of its cavern, selfish, impenetrable, unkind.

'Hi,' says Josh, walking in. And I mumble:

'Hi.'

'Hi,' he mimics in my little voice, and laughs, and still in that little voice he asks, 'What's wrong with you?'

I sigh. I tell him, 'I don't know.'

'I don't know,' he says, getting into bed with me and laughing. 'Poor Lily. Luckily, I've got something in my bag for you.'

Josh is the keeper of the camera which records my life in pictures. And even on excursions of mine which haven't involved him, I've taken my photos at the end of his film. He gets them developed in duplicate.

It's funny, but there's never *really* been the need to do this – from mutual memories we've each of us chosen separate prints. Our albums have become, accidentally, complementary halves of each other, most rewarding when we look at them together.

Tonight, he pulls from out of his bag thirty-six pictures of wonderful moments last summer: the garden in technicolour; the two of us defacing the paving with chalk; the all-but-washed-away backgammon board (so bright back then); Shirley by her hollyhock; that day we went to the seaside with Garry; Edward and I on a walk . . .

'But this one,' he says, 'is the only one I really hoped would come out – and it has.'

It's mr faceless, caught by the zoom lens, ten yards from his house.

'He's bald!' I say.

'I know,' says Josh, and laughs.

We'll put it on the mantelpiece until the joke wears thin. And then it'll go in that drawer full of photos we can't bear to throw away, but don't want to stick in our albums. I sometimes think that drawer is more representative, that those not-so-in-focus, not-so-pretty, so-beautifully-framed rejects much more clearly reflect how it is. But that's not what photo albums are about. Photo albums are Art.

Josh and I update our two this evening. It's a long time since we've done this hand in hand. I like it – sitting on the ground surrounded by two books of paper and photos and sticky white glue with a brush in its lid. There's something so final about storing your memories physically – neatly fixing them in and writing the date and turning the page. In a way, I wish I'd a picture of Colin. But then, I wouldn't stick it in my album, even if I did.

'So, did you blow him out?' says Josh; and I'm about to sigh 'yes' when the telephone rings. We look at each other – don't answer it – and Colin leaves a message. He says, 'Lily – if you don't want to see me again, that's fine. But would you just call me and tell me that? Thanks. Bye.'

'What for?' I ask Josh.

'You should have done it in the first place.'

'But I didn't and it can't make any difference now. What, should I ring him and say, "Hello, I'm not sure if you've realised this, but actually I don't want to see you again"?'

'It's not that,' says Josh, 'He wants to know the reason.'

Yes well, we all want to know The Reason. I'd like to know the reason why I ever met Colin at all. I mean, perhaps I attach undue importance to irrelevant events, but why else would he have appeared in such bizarre and unlikely circumstances if not to play some sort of part from here on in? Was it fanciful of me to imagine this? I don't think so. I'd like to know why the ideas which go on in my head – which aren't obscenely ridiculous – are more rewarding than what really goes on. I'd like to know why I didn't like him. Why not, and who is in control?

Poor Colin, though. I imagine it's worse for him. I imagine his friends saying things like, 'she's not worth it, mate', and, 'she must have some kind of problem'. Then, it's strangely painful imagining this. Because I remember the similar things my friends said to me about the cupboard-man – but I am worth it, I think, I don't think that I've got a problem – so the only reason that a person behaves cruelly, or unkindly, or bizarrely must be that it's you they've woken up next to. It's you. And it isn't Somebody Else.

Is that The Reason also? Once, complaining to Edward about this-and-that, he annoyed me by saying, 'You can't have your cake and eat it.'

I said, 'Why not? Loads of people do.'

He said, '*You* can't have your cake and eat it.'

I know what he's talking about now. That's just the way the story goes – my story anyway – and that's all there is to it. And perhaps if Colin had chosen the girl he'd seen on the bus, and not on the train, hers might have been more interesting.

'What on earth are you on about?' asks Shirley, when I tell her this theory.

'It's just that things don't seem to happen to me.'

'Things like what?'

'Exciting things.'

She snorts, and takes away the pot of tea she's made me. She says, 'Would you like something stronger?' and opens her cupboard. (When you've alcohol in your house like that, that's when you know you're an adult.)

I say, 'A gin and tonic would be delicious.'

But I'm feeling slightly nervous. I only came round here to drop off a toy that Oliver left, I didn't expect I'd get this urge to spill my guts. But I'm just in that mood where I want to tell her – everything I'm thinking about. (And I'm going to feel worse when she doesn't *quite* get what I mean.) And it's not just the theory I'm going to tell her, but the practice as well, the trivial events. I'm about to arm her with details she'll use to reform her opinion of me.

Knowledge is power.

She says, 'Good idea. I'll have one too.'

While she's pouring them, I feel myself prepare to tell the story. I realise I've not told it to anyone else, not in its entirety. I say, 'Remember that day when you and Andrew went off to see a house you liked and I looked after Oliver?'

'Er – not really.'

'It had subsidence or something.'

'Oh, that one! That was ages ago. In the summer.'

'Yeah. Well, that evening, me and Josh –'

'Josh and I.'

'– whatever – we went to a party. And I didn't even *want* to go.'

'Why not?'

'Oh, I don't know. I just didn't. Not in the slightest. But I did go and it was really good fun, and Josh and *I*, we stayed there until about six in the morning and then we came home on the first train.'

'Slightly the worse for wear, I imagine.'

'Very much the worse for wear. I was still completely – drunk, basically. Slightly confused . . . Anyway, we got off the train and just as we were coming up the escalator, this man ran after me and pushed a note in my hand.'

'A note?'

'Yeah. He ran up the escalator, pushed a note in my hand, ran back down and got on the train again.'

'How extraordinary.'

'I know.'

'What did it say?'

'His name and number.'

'No.'

'Yes.'

'What was his name?'

'Colin.'

'Go on.'

'Anyway, I didn't do anything about it.'

'I should hope not.'

'But then . . .'

'Oh, no. Lily!'

'No – nothing bad happened. My life was rolling along

in the same old way and summer was nearly over and I just thought "why not?"'

'I could tell you lots of reasons why not.'

'I know, but in a way you have to do these things, don't you? Just in case. So I called him up.'

'And did he remember you?'

'Of course. He said he'd noticed me on the train before, and I just thought it was a real coincidence. I mean, how often do you see the same person on the train more than once? Especially someone you fancy?'

'But you'd never noticed him?'

'No.'

'So you didn't fancy him?'

'I guess I can't have done, no. Anyway, I still thought it was a real coincidence – more so because it was so early in the morning, you know, an unusual time to travel. I was coming back from a party I hadn't even wanted to go to, he was on his way to the mainline station to catch another train home to his parents' . . .'

'"It was meant to be."'

'Something like that. Anyway, we chatted and he seemed – nice – and he asked if I wanted to meet up and I said yes, and he said we should go to that fair that's on in the summer.'

'Oh, good idea.'

'I know. I kinda liked him for that. It wasn't dinner or a drink – but actually I do remember thinking that he'd come up with that suggestion fairly quickly. I mean, almost as if he'd used it before.'

'Well, he did have quite some time to think of it.'

'Did he?'

'Between giving you the note and you calling him up.'

'Oh yeah.'

'But still, good for him.'

'Yeah. So, the day came – I'd arranged a Saturday afternoon when the fair would be crowded, just in case.'

'Good.'

'And Josh said he'd call me from time to time to make sure I was okay.'

'Good.'

'So off I went. And we met up. And we did have a really good time.'

'Was he handsome?'

'Yes. Well, he wasn't ugly. Not in the least bit.'

'And you got on well?'

'Yes. Well, you know, we got on. He was sweet, actually. Really sweet. And it had been such a long time since I'd been out on a date or kissed anyone. I remember there was one ride we wanted to go on with only two seats left and a little boy in front of us – and his parents said, "Let that couple take those seats and wait till the next one," and, you know. "Couple." It just made me tingle a bit.'

Shirley smiles.

'So yes. Kind of in the context of the day and the place and the complete alienation from our usual lives, we got on.'

'And got off?'

'And got off – a little bit – on the waltzer, and afterwards, and as we were saying goodbye. Just, little kisses. Just quite sweet ones.'

'Ah! What a lovely day.'

'It was a lovely day . . .'

'So what's the problem?'

'Then, he didn't call me for two weeks.'

'Oh. Why not?'

'I don't know. I never asked him.'

'Why?'

'Because *I* never called *him*.'

'Yes, but it doesn't work like that.'

'Well, there wasn't any obligation for him to call me. I mean, either you want to or you don't. And anyway, I didn't want to look like I cared. But of course I did care. I went slightly mad for a while, you know: "What's wrong with me?" "What did I do?" "I thought it had all gone so well" – those kinds of things.'

'Perhaps he already had a girlfriend.'

'Do you think so?'

'Perhaps – you just never know, do you?'

'No, I guess not. I've been so possessive over this whole thing I forgot it was his story too. And perhaps he had a girlfriend . . . Or whatever.'

'Or perhaps he gives his number to all the girls he sees on the train.'

'Perhaps. And there I was thinking I was special.'

'Anyway.'

'Yes. But anyway he did call me and I was really pleased to hear from him because I'd been thinking about him so much, and we went to the cinema.'

'And what did you see?'

'Can't remember. Something. But you know, when we came out he wanted to talk about it straight away, and I always like ten minutes or so to let it settle . . .'

'Mmm.'

'But we talked about it anyway – and we didn't disagree or anything – I mean, there wasn't anything to disagree on. It was kind of a bland film.'

'His choice?'

'Yes.'

'So, you went for a drink?'

'No. I don't know why, but we didn't think of going for a drink. We sort of wandered around aimlessly, so he suggested going back to his place for dinner.'

'Of course he did. I hope you didn't go.'

'I did go.'

'Lily!'

'Which was maybe a bit stupid. But – you know.'

'Yes. I suppose I do.'

'Anyway, we got there and he cooked pasta and I sort of sneaked a look around.'

'Was it nice?'

'Yeah. It was interesting. He had lots of little things everywhere and drawings by friends of his and stuff. But I just got that "What am I doing here?" feeling. I had a bit of an out-of-body experience. You know? I've suddenly transplanted myself into someone else's life and I don't think I want to be here.'

'Yes.'

'It was all a bit – I don't know. I just didn't care. About him or his flat or anything he told me about himself.'

'So you came home?'

'. . . Yes.'

'And that was it?'

'No. Then he called me every day for two weeks and I ignored him.'

'Every day?'

'Yes.'

'There's something wrong with him.'

'Do you think so?'

'Who calls anyone every day for two weeks? I mean, unless they're in love. And he can't have been in love with you. No offence, but he doesn't know you.'

'No.'

'You were never in his life.'

'No. But eventually I called him back, because it's shit isn't it? I hate it when people do that to me.'

'And what did you say.'

'I arranged to meet him. But when it came to it I couldn't face it, so I blew him out.'

'And?'

'And that's it.'

'So?'

'So what?'

'So why don't you think exciting things happen to you?'

'Because –'

'That's quite exciting.'

'Is it?'

'Some guy finds you so attractive he gives you his number . . .'

'You said he did that to all the girls.'

'Conjecture. Some guy runs after you, gives you his number – even though you're with another man . . .'

'Only Josh.'

'Still. Then he takes you to the fair – which I don't expect you've been to before, have you?'

'No.'

'Well, that's exciting.'

'I suppose so, yeah. But pointless.'

'Does that matter?'

'Yes. Because now my life just begins all over again as though nothing's happened. It just carries on as normal.'

'But it's quite nice your life, isn't it?'

'Is it?'

'What, living in your lovely house with Josh, being in this city and being young and going out whenever you want to, having a job that you're good at – and when it all gets too much, getting whisked off to the country by that posh friend of yours?'

'Mmm.'

'I wouldn't mind, if I were you, that my life just carried on as normal.'

* * *

She's right. And something anxious is gone again. It's Friday night. Edward and I are off to the country. Me and my posh friend Edward. Stuck in our usual traffic jam.

six

There's only one game that Lily likes to play and that's the Word Game. The only game she's good at. I *have* tried to get her keen on Risk – you'd have thought she'd have loved Risk. Wouldn't you? You *would* have thought she'd have loved it. She says she objects to it. She says, 'all that strategic planning and scheming and forming alliances, all that fighting for total control,' she says it's not good for her. Fact is, she should play it more often. That's the point of games. I should tell her.

She won't play Backgammon with me either. Pretends she's no time for it. Bridge, Chinese Checkers – she won't even play Croquet. The only game she's got a chance of winning is the Word Game and that's the game we stick to. She says, '. . . journeys are the only times that justify games,' and thinks I think she believes this. Lily talks absolute shit.

It's a good thing then that I taught her the Word Game or else it'd be absolute shit all the way home! That's over three hours!

But does it deserve its capital letters, Word Game? word game? What a disaster if you're the guy who made it up. No way to patent it, police its copyright and make a profit. Unless you had Word Game Patrol stationed in traffic – and even then – unless every car was fitted with a Word Game bugging device.

Here's how you play – and if you *are* the guy who made it up, I'm sorry, but you were onto a lost cause. May as well make your motive altruistic (perhaps it was) a gift you gave to the world. May as well thank me for spreading the word and talk to yourself about karma. You can play this game with any number of people but the fewer the better unless they're quick. You start with someone saying a letter, any letter, suppose it's:

'o'.

I might say 'o' and Lily might say 'o-a' – but she could have said anything at this point, and she could have put it before the 'o' if she'd wished; she could have said 'l-o' (as in piLot) – the point is, we're making a word:

'o'

'o-a'

and each of us is adding a letter on one end or the other (never in the middle), creating this word like a strand of DNA – but both of us having the perverse objective not to be the one to finish it off.

'o'

'o-a'

'b-o-a'

I might say; and you might say – *but you've finished it,*

'*boa*' *is a word*. Not in Word Game speak, the game would never get started. There are just too many combinations of three letters which, while forming part of a word, form a whole word as well, so in Word Game speak, three letters equals three letters, it never equals a word. Lily knows this. She's an old hand. She says:

'D-B-O-A'.

See what I mean? 'D-B-O-A'. Very clever. Some fusions of letters seem surprising at first glance and D-B is one of them. P-B another, C-K-W, N-D-B, N-L-I (I could go on; I caught Lily out some months ago with the T-H-M in the middle of asthma) – one doesn't automatically consider 'cupBoard' or 'backwards', 'handBag' or 'unlikely', but luckily I've been playing this game for some time now and most of the tricks that Lily knows are tricks I've taught her. 'D-B-O-A' wouldn't faze me.

If it had fazed me, if I couldn't think of any word containing those letters and in that order, I could suppose that Lily was trying to fool me, that she had no word in mind at all and I could say, 'Challenge'. Then, if she *was* talking nonsense it'd be one life down for her; but it's a risk calling, 'Challenge', for if she *did* have a word in mind, one life down for me. See, this game doesn't just tax your vocabularian skills but your cunning as well. All my kids will be forced to play.

'O'
'O-A'
'B-O-A'
'D-B-O-A'

?? Oh yes, 'D-B-O-A-R'

And now the game speeds up because now we're limited to a very few words.

'D-B-O-A-R-D'

says Lily, and I come back with, quick as you like:

'R-D-B-O-A-R-D'

And now she's lost.

Not that she'd realise. Not that she wouldn't pronounce:

'A-R-D-B-O-A-R-D'

with a look of victory on her face, a look which says, 'You have no choice but to finish the word'. See Lily presumes that what goes on in her head goes on in everyone else's – but it doesn't (thank god) – like here, you see, she's thinking of 'cardboard' – which she says has no plural – whereas I'm making 'hardboard' which certainly has.

'A-R-D-B-O-A-R-D-S'

Four – two. Me to start. 'z.'

Lily and I have been friends for ten years. Nine, actually, but I say ten because ten has more weight . . . I'm not sure why – eleven has no more weight than ten – perhaps it's because of our fingers and toes. Anyway, Lily and I have been friends for nine years but I've rounded it up to give it more weight because that's what it deserves. Lily is my best friend.

Not that I'd ever say that to her face. Of course not. SHOW, NOT TELL, the teachers used to write in the margins of my essays and it seems to have stuck. Neither do I think she's the most fantastic girl who walks the earth

– I love her . . . in spite of all the things I think about her (which I *would* say to her face) and this is entirely mutual.

All the things I think about her. All the things I think. It's interesting, isn't it, noticing the mechanism. Here I am, 10.30 Sunday morning, still in bed, enacting some . . . peculiarly bland communion in my head with Lily, and why is that? We *did* speak earlier, but it's not *that* conversation I'm replaying.

Here I am, 10.30 Sunday morning and Anna is asleep beside me. So it was yesterday. So will it ever be. I wake up. Anna stays asleep. I watch Anna. Déjà vu . . . When she wakes up I'm going to pretend I've just awoken too, although wake 'up' is not exactly what I mean. I don't mean that quick transition into consciousness, that open-your-eyes-and-you're-ready-for-the-day; I mean that *slow* transition; when the time before you bridge the gap lasts ages; dozing, I suppose you'd call it. Dozing's more fun when you're not alone. But I'm not dozing this morning. I'm wide awake and Anna's fast asleep, I'm watching her. It's not quite as good as dozing but still, it's still quite good.

That's not what Anna looks like, you see. That's Pure Anna. Smoothed, without the creases of the day. There's just so much you'll never know about a person. The person who lives in there. That show for which I'll never get a ticket. Her face is the screen on which she projects the film of her dream (or rather, her face is the screen on which *I* project the film of her dream) but it's not altogether satisfactory. I must make up its plots from smiles and frowns, fill in the gaps between a twitch or a quiver and wonder if she dreams of me.

That girl's propensity to keep unconscious! This morning I've cuddled her, stroked her back, blown on her face, all to no great effect – she's stuck fast. The body reacts, but not to *me*. She started talking earlier, which I foolishly thought meant she was back, but it was sleep-talk, mumbled, 'espresso?' . . . 'no, but that's my sister' . . . one half of a crossed wire. When she said, 'I don't think I can do that', I responded right in her ear, in a loud breathy voice, thinking that'd definitely wake her. But no, what fat was to the Spratts, sleep is in this relationship. 'You can't do what?' I never found out. Nor who she thought she was speaking to in there – only, it certainly wasn't me out here without my passport, talking long-distance and persuading her to join me (the longest distance but one – a taste of what's to come).

That I have never woken up the later, Lily says is a sign my love is stronger. But what would Lily know? She called at nine, can you believe it? Nine on a Sunday! Like I wouldn't prefer to be lying in bed dozing off again. Like I wouldn't prefer to be watching my girlfriend. I said 'For God's Sake!' and she said:

'Come on, I know you've been awake for hours.'

'But Anna hasn't.'

'No, and she won't be either.'

I said, 'You're such a freak. Why are you ringing so early?' and she said:

'Because we're going for a walk this afternoon.'

'It's nine o'clock in the morning!'

'I know. I was wondering if you'd come to pick me up.'

'What.'

'Well, *you've* got a car.'

'No, I meant "What?" kind of excuse is that?'

'Sorry?'

'Anyway – no!'

'Why not?'

'Your house is in the opposite direction.'

'I know – but, Edward, *you've* got a *car*.'

'So you think I should drive for half an hour, pick you up, turn around. Drive for another forty-five minutes – probably getting stuck in traffic –'

'It won't take that long.'

'– while it'd take you fifteen minutes to get here on the underground . . .'

'It doesn't take fifteen minutes.'

'. . . and you wouldn't have to do anything apart from sit down?'

'Edward, I just can't face the underground.'

'Why not? What's wrong with it? You might have to sit next to someone? Someone *normal*?'

'What are you talking about?'

'Stop being such a princess.'

'But I *am* a princess!'

'You're coming round here at twelve o'clock,' I said, in a stern voice, 'and we're going to have lunch. And *then* we're going for a walk in the park. Okay?'

'Okay.'

'A lovely lunch which I'm going to make for you and then a lovely walk which I'm going to drive you to.'

'Okay.'

'More than okay, I'd say.'

'Yes. You're right. Much more than okay.'

'So that's settled is it?'

'Yes, Eddie.'

'Good. Then I'm going back to bed.'

But by the time I'd got there Anna had changed the reel. She was lying absolutely still with her elbows at ninety degrees and her hands in her hair, casually tangled, like she was sunbathing. She *was* sunbathing. I thought *and now I'll never find out what it is that you think you can't do* (and) *trust Lily to deny my denouement.* And then I thought *why is it Anna and not Lily?* (and – just as pertinent) *why is it Lily, not Anna?* And then an overload of scrambled images, which were somehow too disturbing to be cogent, of Lily and Anna as themselves but playing each other's parts, until my brain found an abstract I could deal with: Lily or Anna in the front of my car, Lily or Anna coming home for the weekend – the difference is tangible, but only as smell – not what we talk about, *how* we talk – Anna and I, we – Lily and I – we – play the Word Game – there's only one game that Lily likes to play and that's the Word Game – the only game she's good at . . . It's interesting, isn't it? Noticing the mechanism. Just *interesting*, though, that's all. That's the mistake that Lily makes.

Anna sighs, as if in agreement. 10.35. I'm going to count to three and then give up on a dozy half an hour together.

I'm going to get up. Run a bath. Make a cup of tea. Wash myself. Put on Sunday's clothes. Go out and buy the papers. Come back. Run another bath and Anna will get up. Wash *herself*. Put on *her* clothes – Saturday night's clothes, now lying in a puddle at the foot of my bed. But she can't put on Saturday night. No, Saturday night is over. And maybe that's why I'm hanging in there waiting for her to wake up, planning on pretending, when she does wake up, that I've just awoken too, that we're both in that *half-way-there* and clinging to each other, not quite Sunday morning, nor yet Saturday night, but a surreptitious *little-day* together; a half day, half awake.

But it doesn't look like it's going to happen. So on the count of three ... one ... two ... She opens her eyes suddenly and sits up, her hands still behind her head (like she's at the gym working on her four-pack), stretches her arms and makes fists, releases them, turns her head ninety degrees and looks at me. Registers. Smiles, says, 'Morning' in a funny accent, and gets out of bed. Walks out of the door. Walks into the bathroom. I hear her turn on one tap and then another, clean her teeth, splash her face and swizzle the water she's running in the bath. When it's full I'll get in with her – it's not the Sunday morning I imagined. It's neither of the Sunday mornings I'd imagined ... but then it's impossible to second guess, and that's not just to do with her – though she's full of surprises – that's just the way it is.

No, I will never be in love like I imagined it. (And for that reason, Lily will *never* be in love.) Like I imagined it was

77

like I imagined university when I was fifteen – a magical, free-form society where everyone had the same goal: To Know. In a similar way, I suppose, I've been disappointed, but only so long as I clung to that thought and wouldn't let go. That moments of 'in love', *mutually*-in-love are as transitory as the songs they inspire; that you can spend hours, days, weeks, watching someone *other* from behind your eyes, watching them watching you behind theirs, and then jump suddenly to the same side – but only for a moment; that you might have the same goal but never the same experience; *that* you can either find sad or you can find beautiful. But that's the way it is.

This week Anna is calling the shots. For no other reason than *I'm* not calling them. That's the way we work. And I cannot be sure, but I more than suppose, that that's the way we all work. Swings and roundabouts. There is a bizarre politic I've noticed in human relationships, all human relationships, not just sexual. It is this: when someone doesn't want you, they're God, but as soon as they do they're unworthy. Perhaps that's too strong, but look at the last few weeks with Anna: I'd been busy, I'd been only sporadically returning her calls, and in response she'd been sending me e-mails, leaving me messages, inviting me to parties; she bought me sweets, sent me jokes in the post – *see me! notice me! think I'm great* – but the more she attempted to show me herself, the more I just revelled in her attention. Like she was my mirror showing me a wonderful reflection; and then she gave up. And the minute she gave up I turned round to find her, only to find her pulling away. It's my turn to chase her this week. This week Anna is calling the shots.

The bath is full, I can hear her getting in. I get up and get in with her. She says, 'Why do you always have to get in *behind* me?' and then, to herself, 'So I have to have the tap end.'

'Actually, I was going to wash your lovely back.'

'Right,' she says, sarcastic, 'Cos it's really, really dirty.'

I wash it anyway.

She says, 'My next bath is going to be a bath for two.'

'Along the same lines as a tandem?'

'Yes. And with no tap end.'

'Don't you quite like the two of us in a bath for one? Like twins?'

She doesn't answer. She gets out. I guess that's an answer.

I say, 'Stay with me a minute.'

'I'm cold.'

'I'll put more hot in.'

She pulls a towel off the radiator and begins to rub herself down.

Ah, Anna. Beautiful Anna. You may be calling the shots, my lover, but today I've got a Joker up my sleeve.

And I'm wondering when to play it. Now, while you apply your moisturiser? Or as you assemble the clothes you've left on my floor? Or later? Once you've settled down to spend the day with me? It is an elastic band between us and there's no point us going in the same direction, I have to stretch the other way and hope we might snap back. So I've arranged to spend the day with someone else – Lily.

Not an altogether random choice, Lily, an old friend of mine who Anna doesn't like. An old friend of mine who knew me before there was Anna, who shares things with me that Anna cannot touch. And it's not that I'd prefer to see Lily today (not this week when I'm playing Mirror), but I've got to get hold of the reins. I want her and I've got to make her want me back. Tactics, strategies and risk. Perhaps tonight we'll have a moment.

I get out of the bath, get dressed, go into the kitchen. Anna's got her back to me, she's looking in the fridge. She says, 'There's a lot of food in here, Eddie. Makes a change.'

'It's for Lily,' I say. And then, casual as anything, 'We're having lunch later – going for a walk.'

Then, one of those seconds which extends like chewing gum . . . that unfolds in slow motion . . . when the conscious mind works like the sub-conscious . . . takes in every bit of information . . . if I were a dolphin I'd see her back muscles stiffen . . . hair follicles contract . . . I *know* that she's cross. But she won't make a fuss (see, she's big on each of us doing our own thing) and I say, 'What are *you* up to today?' (which presumes she's a life of her own . . . which lets her regain her composure . . .) she says, 'Oh, I don't know. Maybe go and see Daisy,' but there's a wobble in her voice, and I nod – without looking smug . . . or like I've won – anything at all . . . but when someone doesn't want you, even for a second . . . I'm God again.

And God can afford to be nice. Make her tea. Make her toast. Butter it. Marmalade? Make like nothing's gone on. But I'm God again!

The doorbell rings half an hour too soon. No matter how hard she tries Lily always comes early, like she's always escaping from whatever she's just been doing. I feel badly, quickly, I've given her a hand in a cardgame of which she's unaware. What does that say of the lives we all think we lead? And she's my friend, and I love her. 'How was your journey?' I say. Kissing her.

'Terrible.'

'You didn't get a carriage all to yourself?'

'No. I had to stand most of the way – and when I did get a seat, it was next to a couple.'

'God how awful.'

'I know. They were all over each other. I don't like to be reminded that I have anything in common with the world at large. Especially that thing.'

'What thing?' asks Anna.

'Sex.'

'Distressing isn't it?' I say, and Lily laughs.

But Anna doesn't. She's thinking *That's the most ridiculous thing I've ever heard.*

After she's gone (she waited ten minutes for decency's sake) I say to Lily, 'So, how are you?'

'Fine.'

'And what've you been up to?'

'You don't have to ask, you know. I know you're only pretending to take an interest.'

'I'm not pretending. I'm always hopeful you're going to tell me something interesting. You very rarely do.'

'That's because you're such an unreceptive audience. You never cut me any slack.'

'Okay, so I'm cutting you some slack now.'

'Actually, quite an interesting thing has happened. A few months ago I went to a party and there was this girl there who I took a bit of an instant dislike to –'

'You see, that's the problem. There's always some long story involved. You can't just get to the point.'

'But, Edward, if I don't tell you the story you'll miss the subtleties of the point. And that's what I mean about you not cutting me any slack. You make me rush towards the end which makes my story boring. I could tell it really well if you'd let me.'

'Well do then.'

'No, I can't with you. It's impossible. It's our politic.'

'Well tell me what you were going to tell me, anyhow you want.'

'I went to a party a few months ago, with Josh. And there at the party was a girl who I took an instant dislike to. For no good reason other than – well, for no good reason. She was wearing a bra-top with an Action Man stuffed down it and real state-of-the-art trainers. I didn't speak to her or anything, but I was introduced to her. She was called Mary. Anyway, I've met her again and she's not hideous at all, in fact, she's my new friend. She's not at all like I imagined.'

'Which only goes to show how wrong your first impression can be.'

'You're so patronising. That wasn't where I was going at all.'

'Where were you going?'

'I was going to tell you about her. Actually, she's rather extraordinary.'

'Lily, they all are.'

'Who?'

'All these people you tell me about. Absolutely extraordinary and absolutely only in your life for five minutes.'

'You shouldn't think I'm not aware of that,' she says slowly, 'you shouldn't think it doesn't depress me.'

This seems like a good opportunity to eat. I take the food out of the fridge and lay it on the table. For a little while we're both pretending everything is fine. 'Oh that looks delicious,' one of us says, 'Oh isn't this lovely?' 'Oh, try one of these.' Finally, between mouthfuls, I say, 'I'm sorry.'

'Don't be.'

'Don't be cross with me.'

'I'm not cross.'

'You are.'

'No. But I would like you to know, it's not always my fault. I mean, sometimes, whether people remain friends or not is nothing to do with the effort they make or don't make, it's something out of their hands.'

'You're right, it is. Sometimes.'

'I enjoy meeting new people and having new experiences. You shouldn't give me a hard time for that.'

It's not really that that I give her a hard time for. But this isn't the moment to explain. It might never be the moment to explain. We should go now, anyway, go for our walk. Safer to be doing something, something to pin a bond on, something to make you forget, for a moment, everything you might not say. I say, 'We should go. It'll be dark before we know it.'

'I can't believe it,' I say, half way there in the car, 'I can't believe this traffic.'

'Why not? We're always stuck here.'

'Not going this way. Not on a Sunday. Where's everyone going?'

'To the park?'

'I could understand it if it was Friday night.'

'Mmm. Every Friday night we rehearse the desertion of the city.'

'Did you just make that up?'

'No, it's something I've been thinking about recently. I always feel a bit apocalyptic in your car on a Friday night.'

'You always feel a bit apocalyptic.'

'Yes, you're right, I do. But don't you?'

'No. Why should I?'

'Because, well . . . how can I explain? You know how the week starts off really, really slowly, and you sort of drag your way through Monday, Tuesday, Wednesday, Thursday morning . . . and then suddenly on Thursday afternoon everyone starts to perk up, I always feel like – I'm not sure which happens first – as soon as everyone starts to perk up, so does time, it starts going quickly, like a roller coaster carrying us all faster and faster, with us all getting more and more excited, whooshing down into the weekend.'

'I like that.'

'Well I feel like it's Thursday afternoon all the time.'

'And you're always a little excited?'

'Yes. But then, it never comes to anything. The weekend becomes the week again. The excitement never manifests.'

Occasionally when you're with people you remember exactly why it is that you love them. The thing which makes them them and drew you to them in the first place. Usually it's the same thing that comes between you, the thing that you might not say. We park the car with the hill out in front of us.

'My god,' says Lily as we walk towards it, 'look at the trees. We really have come on a perfect day, a perfect autumn day . . . Last time we were here,' she says, 'it was August. Funny.'

'What's funny about that?'

'Impossible to feel the heat of it now,' and then, 'So much beauty and joy in all this death.'

'Well, I guess it knows it's going to come back.'

'Yes, but not *this* leaf, *this* flower.'

I say, 'You know, Lily, we've made up time, made up millennia, made up week and weekend. Your feeling of apocalypse, your excitement, your bored depression is based on something that doesn't exist.'

'Of course I know that,' says Lily, 'but it doesn't matter. The fact is, I have the thought.'

'Well have another one. Make an effort. Do something.'

'You said exactly the same thing in August, and I did. I rang some random guy who gave me his number. We went out. I was completely prepared to like him. I was. I'd mentally made a space for him in my life. But when it came to it, there was nothing between us. Nothing at all. You say that people come and go in my life in five minutes and that's true but the fact is that's how life is. Unfair. Dangles a carrot.'

'How many times did you meet?'

'Nothing means anything. It's all just random, pointless interactions. We went our separate ways, my life resumed itself, it might as well not have happened.'

'How many times did you meet?'

'Twice.'

'Twice?' I say, suddenly getting angry with her. 'You pretend that you want your interactions with people to have some meaning, you say you'd like to have some direction, but you don't really. If you did you'd do things differently. You would have met this man again, for instance. But you spend your whole time looking for something new to excite you without ever building on what you've got. You want answers when you don't even know what the question is. You're after an easy fix.'

seven

But perhaps I shouldn't berate Lily too much for her taste for adventure, everyone has their drug. Antiques, art, food, sex, melancholy, melodrama, God, music, money, coins, stamps, parties, movies, families – drugs – whatever. What's yours? Living is all about greed and desire; Life Is consuming your drug.

If you're *homo sapiens*, that is. The others seem quite happily self-contained . . .

But the other animals need only survive, Man's instinct is to extend himself. I'd blame thumbs, only apes have them too, and my theory doesn't apply to apes. But I'm sure thumbs have something to do with it. If you've got thumbs, you don't have to *be* things, you can make them. Instead of evolving strength, you can make a spear. I've often thought that if you can make a fax machine you could be a fax machine, that if you can speed matter up, turn it to sound, transport it across the airwaves, slow it down again, turn it back into matter, surely you could do it with the matter that is you, but perhaps that's going too far, but you see what I mean? Instead of being something, you make it, ergo, whatever you need is outside you, whatever you want is outside you, ergo, extension of self. Perhaps thumbs created God? What is it that makes the rich man keep on making money? He has to have something he doesn't yet have, he has to have something beyond him. If extension of self is innate, desire is innate. And you cannot desire what you already have. You can appreciate it, sure, but you cannot desire it.

Perhaps this is the politic at work between me and Anna. As soon as I haven't got you, I want you, as soon as I have you, I can no longer desire you . . . But I could appreciate you.

Incidentally, it worked, that little trick I pulled with Lily. Sunday evening I rang Anna and she was only too pleased to hear from me. She was even more pleased to hear that Lily had annoyed me. She took me out to dinner. We went to bed early.

All's been well since then, we are having a honeymoon period. This weekend I am taking her home, just her, my parents are away. Autumn's in full bloom (bloom?) and I thought I could cash in on this romantic mood of ours before it splits.

It takes three hours to drive home and an hour and a half of that is just leaving the city. Last night I heard on the radio that cars in this city move at an average of eight miles an hour – that's just slower than a cart and horse. Apparently, at the advent of the motorcar, people were thrilled. This new way of moving, they thought, would be clean. ! No more horseshit polluting the air. But that's what all our good intentions come to. Inventions thwart themselves. We speed things up only to slow ourselves down.

This particular piece of road is going to be widened. The council has bought the houses, boarded them up and is waiting to knock them down. But one or two idiots, one or two irritating idiots, are holding onto their horrible houses (as though anyone wants a view of the traffic) and holding the whole thing up. They'll lose, of course. No point fighting the machine. But until they do this road remains too narrow. Oh for the day when they're moved away and the bulldozers moved in.

'We won't get there until ten o'clock at this rate,' I say. 'Look at it. Stop, start, stop, start,' and then, 'It's a metaphor.'

'What for?'

'Life. Mind you, it'd be more like life if it were hilly.'

'But then it would be a simile.'

'Don't get clever.'

'Anyway, it doesn't need to be hilly. Start is downhill and stop is uphill.'

'No. Start is when you're on the up and stop is when you're coming down.'

'Start is when you're at the top and stop is when you're at the bottom.'

'It doesn't matter where start or stop are, all that matters is that they're there.'

'It's tiring, huh?'

'Mmm.'

'Do you think you ever get to the home run?'

'Don't know. Don't think so. It always feels like the home run until you stop again.'

But then it doesn't matter, for every time you start you forget what stasis is like.

Anna turns on the radio, starts singing, out of tune. I've never told her that her singing annoys me and now it's too late. Still, it gives her pleasure. It worries me, the myriad things I've never told her (and I wonder, what has she never told me?) and how easy it might be to let them all come out one day, in the heat of a fight, and how easy it would be to destroy this relationship. But it's much easier to destroy all things than to build them. See? The odds are stacked against us.

I had a fight with a vicar last week. 'Not a fight,' he said, 'a *discussion*', but I was fighting. I said, 'Don't you think that monogamy is unnatural?' He said, 'Yes. That's what makes it Divine.' But is it divine or just wishful thinking? There are millions of people out there, millions and millions, and how beautiful to think that there's one meant for you. Just for you. For me.

Because otherwise, love is manmade and marriage convenient. I think of all those people over all those centuries who just did it, just got on with it, for power, for land, for children, for security, to please their parents ... and only very rarely for love.

My parents have gone away for a romantic weekend of their own. It is unusual in this century to have parents still together and I'm lucky. But I still say they're wrong for each other. They hate it when I say that. My mother has prepared all the food Anna and I will need for the next two days and all Anna has to do is put it in the oven. (She kicks me when I tell her this.) There's a lasagna for supper tonight and a treacle tart, sausages for breakfast, pâté for lunch, trout for the evening and a roast for Sunday. Potatoes already peeled, parboiled and scratched with a fork, in a roasting dish, in oil. 'You're so spoiled,' says Anna, and I say, 'She hasn't done it for me. Mothers like to feel useful.'

We play Scrabble after supper. I thrash her, hands down. My ideal woman beats me every time. But really, she prefers to play Risk.

Saturday morning is drizzly. I wake up, as usual, 7 a.m. As usual, Anna sleeps on. There are so many things that aren't right between us, but perhaps everyone who isn't you is other, and is hard to spend your time with. Perhaps as soon as you let go of your dream of perfection, perhaps as soon as you realise that the one for you is you and anyone else is weird, odd, strange (has to be by their very definition), perhaps then . . .

I go out and buy the papers, come back and read them over sausages. Anna sleeps on. I'm not really reading. I'm thinking about Anna and me and whether we should split up. Is the reason we stay together because it's less painful than splitting up? We are good together, me and Anna, but I don't know if I want to spend the rest of my life with her. But how does anyone know that? When I was single (and God! I was single for years before I met Anna) I longed for a girlfriend. And now that I've got one, I've found the desire is still there. I'm still waiting for my perfect partner. But is this because Anna and I are wrong for each other? Or because I've got thumbs? And is that vicar right about monogamy or is there a perfect person out there? Can't be, can there?

I'd like to go for a walk to clear my head but the drizzle has turned to a storm. I go for a walk round the house instead. Lily has never had a house, a continuing house, Lily has never had a home. Her father, some sort of travelling salesman (although she's never specific) moved every few years and took her and her mother with him. They shed their skins, left behind, sold or threw away everything they couldn't fit in their car. Their two-door car. No exercise books full of five-year-old's drawings, no ancient cuddly toys, no cute outfits that she used to wear to parties . . . and it suddenly comes to me, it's not adventure she's after, though she thinks it is, it's home. Poor Lily, I think. And suddenly I love her.

My whole life is contained in this house, this attic is like seventeen junk shops. Little blue coats we used to wear to school, all our old toys, posters, pop memorabilia of bands we were into, family photos, old curtains, old china – I remember that tea set – old lamps, old rugs. So many incarnations I've had, and all here, and where to next and is it time to move on? Sometimes I think, what am I doing still coming here every weekend possible?

I say this to Anna this evening and she says, 'Don't be

silly, what else would you do? Where else would you go?'

I don't know.

I'm not going to let her sleep on today. We hardly ever spend any time on our own and I want to make the most of it. Usually it's busy, busy, busy and we only get ourselves to ourselves at the end of an evening and first thing the next morning when it's either rush off to work or watch her sleeping. No, I'm not going to let her sleep on today. It's a beautiful day. Sun shining, autumn leaves right at their peak. If we'd come a week later we'd have missed them.

I've yet to meet my match when it comes to walking; Anna traipses after me, complaining, tells me that her blood sugar levels can't keep up with this nervous energy of mine. But walking makes me feel better. Man is nomadic. This land is the land I know best, I've been walking it all my life. New owners come and new owners go, move the footpaths, take down stiles, grow hedges, but they'll never put me off, I go everywhere, anywhere. This land feels like mine. I tell Anna I'm taking her up the hill where we can see the line of cedars. She says, 'I've seen them before,' but I love the proud composure of cedars and even Anna is amazed by the view from the top. Oaks, chestnuts, maples, all showing off. 'Green, red, orange, gold, brown,' she says. She says, 'It won't be like this for long.'

No, it won't be like this for long. The air still. Still warmish. The leaves adding their decoration to the trees. The trees will soon be stark like bones without them. I say, 'I want to take a picture.'

'We haven't got a camera.'

'In my mind,' I say.

'Yes,' says Anna, 'to keep against your heart.'

'To warm my heart,' I say, putting my arm around her, 'against the coming cold.'

She says, 'From up here it's like a learn-a-language text book.'

'Huh?'

'You know, like the ones you get at school. With pictures of loads of people all doing different things. There's a couple pushing a pram, there's a man walking his dog, there's a woman –'

'Who are we?'

'We're . . .'

'We're the Young People,' I say.

'Not so young,' says Anna.

'No,' I say, 'not so young.' And then, 'What do you think is worse, regretting the things you do or regretting the things you don't do?'

She kisses me. She says, 'Edward, sometimes I really, really love you.'

Sometimes. Perhaps all you ever get is sometimes.

'Anna,' I say, 'will you marry me?'

eight

I have always been big. Big bones, big bottom, big mouth, big head. Big hair! I could have added 'big plans' once upon a time but I don't have any of those these days. Small ones, shopping lists, things to do: the house to run, Oliver to feed, clothe, drive about, Andrew to love. Sounds like I don't love Ollie there, doesn't it? but I do, but in a different way. I have always believed you should love your spouse more than your child for your spouse will always be with you. No such luck for my mother, though, my daddy died when I was eleven months old, my mum and I have survived on tales of him for thirty-eight years. He must be mainly fiction by now. The most handsome man you ever saw, although, perhaps this much is true. I've seen his picture. But it is easy for the dead, they do no wrong. Best friend, best husband, the biggest man who ever lived, never mind that he did away with himself and left us stranded . . .

Strangely, my mum felt no anger about this, or perhaps she did, perhaps she just didn't tell me. She used to say, when I asked where he was, 'Oh, darling, he's in heaven'

and when I asked how he got there, 'he took too many of
the wrong pills'. I was thirteen before I worked this out.
Took 'too many of the wrong pills' literally, as though there
could be a right one. Wrong ones were pink? blue? green?
but not white, not like the ones she used to dissolve in a
cup of too much water and make me take to cure all ills.
'I've sprained my ankle', 'I've cut my knee', 'I've broken
my heart', those dreadful words: aspirin gargle and swallow.
Aspirins were the right pills and how I longed to take the
wrong ones, too many of the wrong ones, and get to heaven,
and find my dad.

I'm glad that Oliver has a Mum *and* a Dad and I pray
things will stay this way. It was when I conceived that I
started to pray and to go to church, it was all my dreams
come true. Couldn't have been a better year for me, that
one, I've had nothing like it since. Thirty-five and still a
spinster, fat, middle-aged and lonely, living in the middle
of a massive city where, you would have thought, there
were plenty of men to spare. But the legions of frogs I
kissed before I found my prince – I've told this to Lily,
I've said, 'there are plenty of fish in the sea, my darling,
but you hold out for a dolphin, I did and look at me.'
Thirty-five and still a spinster (so much more frightening
than bachelor, that word, almost spider, almost sinister,
sinister spider, spinster) and fat and lonely and then there
was Andrew. I bless that 'there'. It was a friend's birthday,
a dinner in some crummy restaurant in town and there he
was sitting opposite, tall dark and mustachioed. He offered
me a lift home, got into my bed and didn't get out until

three days later; proposed after six, married me within a month and made me pregnant before you could say 'contraceptive'. I started going to church. You have to say thank you to someone, haven't you?

And besides, once Ollie was born, I found it a comfort. It was like, here is my family, and I put it inside a bigger family, and God keeps his arms around us. You have to suspend your disbelief but I've learnt not to ask too many questions – virgin birth, son of God, heaven and hell, Sinning, the holy trinity, Jesus dying for the likes of me, resurrecting Himself, walking on water – you mustn't probe, probing spoils things, probing gets you . . . like Lily, unsure, unhappy.

I went round there yesterday and she and Josh were writing their Christmas cards. They make their own every year, which I think is a waste of paper and paint and glitter when they could be spending that money on charitable cards and raising some cash for children. Or the homeless, or unlucky animals. I've told them what I think but still they make their own cards, the same cards as though they're a couple (they'd make a lovely couple), this year a white potato-print angel on dark blue paper. It's Josh with the artistic talent, Lily just adding their halos with a silver glitter-pen, but she looked daggers when I said this. Some people just won't hear the truth. And she's one. Didn't even offer me a cup of tea once I'd said this and I had to make my own. But I think she was in a bad mood before I arrived. She was up to E on her list. 'E for Edward,' she said, and added, 'I suppose I'll have to write it jointly from now on, to him *and* Anna,' in a certain truculent tone. They're getting married and she's never liked Anna. Had her eye on Edward herself, I think, and that house in the country, and his family whom she treats as her own. Although the way she does treat her own is shocking. Hardly ever a visit, hardly ever a phone call and never a mention, even when asked. 'How are your parents, Lily,' I might say, and she'll say something like, 'Hideous'. They seemed far from hideous when I met them. Old, yes, parochial, maybe, disapproving of Josh, certainly, but who can blame them? You worry, don't you? when it comes to your children, I'd worry if I knew no better and how are they supposed to know? He's a lovely boy Josh, but how are they supposed to know? Different generation. She's refusing to go home this Christmas, and she ought to, and she's an only child too. Yes, it's important to love your spouse more than your child for your spouse will always be with you. If you're lucky.

Although, being brought up without a father has had its advantages. It's meant I don't play to roles. I might conform to them but I don't play to them and if I do conform to them then that's because it's the way things are. Andrew does the manly things and I do the girly things but it's not role-playing, it's because we're good at them. I've never had a father to change the bulb or mend the fuse or build a fence in the garden but I'm glad I've a husband to. I got one out of ten for changing a plug in a physics lesson and my skills lie elsewhere. I'm a nurturer. I'm a natural mother. I can cook like you wouldn't believe, I can clean,

I can comfort and I am content to let Andrew bring home the cash. It's important to let your man feel like a man. Women forget that in these days of 'liberation'.

It's only two weeks till Christmas and I've been left behind, no cards, no presents, no tree, no turkey, no chocolate, no nothing, I must make a list. Oliver goes to nursery these days, which is a relief (although I feel guilty saying so) because I don't have him under my feet all day getting bored or tetchy or making a mess of the house. He's a funny child. Quite quiet and secretive and it'd do him good to have a brother or a sister but we've tried and tried and nothing will take. Too old now, probably, too overweight. Christmases are different since he's come along, I see the point of them now. That first Christmas Andrew and I spent together, that was the best one I'd had since I stopped believing in Santa Claus. I was six months pregnant. We spent all Christmas Eve in bed under the duvet, Andrew running downstairs from time to time to fetch me toast or tea or some daft present he'd secretly hidden. We had a disposable income then. We gave each other our presents on Christmas Eve, keeping just one back for the following day, for the following day, both sets of parents were coming for lunch and they wouldn't approve of such stupid extravagance. Andrew's parents are mean and have no excuse. My mother's mean, but that's because she's always been counting her pennies, putting coppers in jars and hiding them so they'd be a surprise when she found them, a happy surprise if they coincided with a bill, which they did sometimes. But not very often.

After I stopped believing in Santa Claus, Christmas seemed pointless. Santa and my father had become inextricably linked – Father Christmas, I suppose – but once I found out he was fiction I stopped getting a stocking and then there were years of just my mum and me waking up on Christmas morning and giving each other our one sad present and wondering how to pass the time before driving to Auntie Mona's for lunch, where we'd munch through too many sweets before dinner and my mum would get drunk. Said she had to, to get through. Auntie Mona and Uncle Tim, their children Peter, Peggy and Tom, Granny and Grandpa, Uncle Tim's parents (who tried to make me call them Annie and Buppa as though I were their own) and me and my mum, and my dead dad, and no Father Christmas. And because she got drunk, we always had to stay longer than the rest for her to sleep it off.

When I got older Peter, Peggy and Tom came less and less often to these lunches, having other halves to go to, and Annie and Buppa died, and so did Granny and then Grandpa, until it was just Mona and Tim, Mummy and me . . . but then I met Andrew.

It is sad that my mum never let anyone love her apart from my dead dad, who could do no wrong. We try to make it up to her, Andrew and I and Oliver, we lavish her, but she's no good at receiving. She says, 'What did you get me this for? It must have cost a fortune!' and I wonder, what would she have been like if he'd never died, would she have been softer? And I wonder, why did he do it? and was it my arrival? or was it her? Why, why, why?

But I don't have these thoughts so often since I met Andrew, since I've had Oliver. Oliver will always get a stocking, even though he looked at me last week and said, 'Mummy, how does Father Christmas go round the whole world in just one night?'

I said, 'Because it's not night at the same time in every country. When it's night here, on the other side of the world it's day.'

He said, 'But it's still a very long way.'

'Well,' I said, 'Father Christmas can make time stand still.'

'How?' he asked.

'By sprinkling magic snowflakes out of his sleigh.'

'Mummy,' he said, 'I don't think I believe you,' so I told him the truth. He didn't seem at all bothered. In fact, he was pleased that it was his mum and his dad who bought him presents and not some stranger whom he'd never meet.

But there are only two weeks to go and I've not bought a thing apart from bits and bobs for Oliver's stocking this morning. I've had a productive day today but until this morning I was taking one step forward and two steps back. Andrew and I are trying to move up to the north of the city and nearer my mum, who lives out in the suburbs. She's getting older and I like to keep an eye on her. This is the house we've lived in since we married and it's suited us perfectly, just far enough out of the centre to be quiet, just near enough in to be convenient. But it's one of those houses that were built too quickly fifty or so years ago, to contain a growing population. Its rooms are small, its walls thin, and although we've been lucky with our neighbours – Lily and Josh on one side, Mr and Mrs Petersham on the other – it's time to move on. The schools are better up north. The park is nearer and, because it's on a hill, the air is cleaner. I want to get Ollie a dog. I want a spare bedroom. I want a bigger garden. I want. I want. I want. Sometimes my prayers are nothing but asking. Do you think God minds? Do you think He says, 'For God's sake be grateful'? For God's sake! It's been my job to find us a house and I'd not done too well till today. Our buyer's getting tetchy. 'Too choosy,' Andrew said, and I said, 'It pays to be choosy, I held out for you,' (then he kissed me) but God couldn't have minded my requests too much, for the estate agent rang last week and said something had come in like he'd never seen before. An absolute bargain, he said. The owner deceased. No chain. A marvel of a little house, he said, older than that part of the city, a country cottage. I didn't believe his jargon – estate agents, I don't know what planet they live on – but as it turned out, it was true. A sweet little cottage, detached, built a couple of hundred years ago, before the city expanded, when that hamlet was not even a suburb but a village. An open fire, a fifty-foot garden, four bedrooms (well, three and a box, but room for a dog), a two-minute walk to the park, and on the market for less than this place. The catch? The plumbing. Lead piping, and it hasn't been decorated since god knows when. Before *I* was born. Still, I took Andrew at the weekend and he loved it, I took Josh this afternoon to quote us on plumbing, re-wiring and decoration, and it isn't as bad as it looks, and tomorrow I'm taking Mr Petersham. Fingers crossed. New year, new house.

Tomorrow I'm taking Mr Petersham and then I've got to get busy. Today's been a productive day but I've got to do better tomorrow. Get up at six instead of just wake up. I always wake up at six, it's a part of the day that I love. The house quiet, Andrew asleep beside me, mouth slightly open, breath showing on his greying mustachio. I asked him to shave it off once but he wouldn't. I asked and I asked and I asked and eventually he did what I wanted. I said, 'You were right,' and he grew it straight back. Funny, his little lip looked, hairless. Lucky that he had the option. His breath shows on his greying mustachio and I put my arm around him and outside the window it's night still. The street lamps shining, the road quiet, I like to imagine the whole street under their duvets, I like to listen for sounds of life: alarm clocks, front doors, ignitions. Oliver's an early riser too and self-sufficient like I am. He can lie perfectly happy in bed staring at that mural on the ceiling – Josh painted that mural – thinking his own little thoughts. I wonder what little thoughts in that little head? Are they 'what'll I do today?' thoughts or 'what did I do last week?' or 'what'll I be when I'm older?'? Who knows? He's a funny child, quiet and secretive.

But that's what I love about him, he's always been his own person. Not mine, not Andrew's, it's like we're just looking after him, like he was supposed to be. Special some-how. But perhaps all parents think that. I get up at six thirty. I go downstairs and I put on the kettle. Andrew likes a cup of tea in bed and a cuddle. Oliver used to come in when he heard us chatting and get under the covers, but since he started nursery he's stopped that. He likes to get dressed like a big boy. Before bedtime we choose his clothes for the following day and I put them on the radiator so they'll be warm for him to get into, and at seven, just as Andrew's extracting himself from my arms and the duvet and moaning how warm it is in there, how cosy, I hear Ollie get up. He's dressed and sitting at the table by the time I go down. Good boy, Oliver, good big boy, but quite strange (but I never say that to his face). He and Andrew like porridge for breakfast in the winter and in the summer they like – porridge. Funny pair. Do you know the secret of porridge? A pinch of salt. Just a pinch. Makes all the difference. Me, though, I never eat breakfast. Before I met Andrew I used to wake up thinking of caffeine and nicotine and it'd be the coffee and the fag, the delicious coffee and fag, that would get me out of bed in the morning. But I stopped them both the moment I knew I was pregnant and it seemed ridiculous to take them up again. Apparently they're appetite suppressants but I've never had much of an appetite. I pick at my food and I've always been big. It's the way I am. My mother's small and thin like a sparrow, but not her daughter with her child-bearing hips. Just the one child, though, but you never know.

This morning, after Andrew left for work and before I took Ollie to nursery, I made a list. 'Now be a good boy, Ollie,' I said, 'and don't disturb Mummy, she's concentrating,' and it occurred to me how odd it is, this habit parents have of referring to themselves in the third person. You'd never do it with a friend would you? I'd never say, 'Hold on a moment, Lily, Shirley's just got to go upstairs and get her handbag.' It's like it points to someone who isn't there. A bigger Mummy than me, than the mummy who's speaking the words. We must do it to boost our authority. I should mention this to Andrew. I should ask if it's a habit worth breaking. Anyway, I made a list, a lovely long list with subsections so there'd be plenty to cross off. Nothing like crossing things off a list. This is what my big plans have come to, small ones, shopping lists, things to do.

But I remember once at school, in a General Studies lesson, we were taught how a person mopping the floor in a factory gains more job satisfaction than the factory worker himself because the floor-mopper can see how much he's done and how much he's got left to do. He can feel pleased with himself at the end of the day (and I use that phrase in its literal sense) by looking at the shining floor, at the wholeness of his job well done. I didn't buy it at the time and I don't buy it now, but I kind of know what was meant. I don't think I'd ever get satisfaction from mopping a floor that wasn't mine, but I do know what was meant. To have a goal and little ways to get to it, this black square then that white one, this row of white squares, that diagonal of black – this is how I feel when I cross things off my list – this one's squeaky, that one's shiny, this one's fresh and that one's clean and then the whole damn floor.

I can cross everything off my list today, I love days like this. One, nursery; tick. Two, bits and bobs for Ollie's stocking; tick: chocolate spiders, tick; crayons, tick; glitter, tick; scrapbook, tick; felt-tips, tick; multi-coloured cotton wool, tick; Sergeant Sam bubble-bath, tick; glue, tick. Three, home; tick. Three A, change sheets on beds; tick. Three B, wash sheets and towels; tick. Three C, dust bedrooms; tick. Three D, dust landing; tick. Three E, water plants; tick. Three F, hoover upstairs; tick. Three G, clean bathroom; tick. Everything looks better when it's clean but where did I get the habit? My mother's filthy. Says the dumps she's always lived in haven't deserved a scrubbing, but everything looks better when it's clean. The meanest shack's more cosy when it's clean. How she copes in her squalor I just don't know, the bathroom grimy, the carpets dusty, the lino in her kitchen sticky. When I was a child I kept my shoes by the bed so my bare feet wouldn't have to touch her floorboards – thank god that I don't live there any more. Four, pick Ollie up from nursery; tick. Five, butcher; tick. Five A, chicken legs; tick. Five B, shoulder of lamb; tick. Five C, mince; tick. Six, home; tick. Six A, fishfingers and peas for Oliver's lunch; tick. Seven, to number 93, Josh.

Number 93 is going to be our new house, if all goes well with Mr Petersham. We've been lucky with our neighbours, Mr Petersham a surveyor on one side and Josh trained as a plumber on the other. He trained as a plumber but works as a painter-decorator. 'Didn't like putting my hands down other people's toilets,' he said when I asked him why this is. Not sure if it was a joke, he's a man of minimal facial expression. Minimal bodily everything, actually, and never speaks unless it's urgent. Any more laid-back and he'd still be asleep. He used to unnerve me when he first moved in but he's a lovely boy behind his spooky stare, those huge eyes he has with their girlish lashes, long like a girl, if she's lucky, but always with a speck of detritus on them which is not like a girl. He's a funny mix, 'Queer,' my mother would say, and she'd be right. But I'm very fond of Josh, strange as he is, he'll put himself out. We went round to the new house today and he 'enthused' and said he'd make an exception for Ollie and me and replace the lead-piping. 'You won't mind putting your hands down our toilets?' I said, but he didn't laugh, he said, 'There's just one condition, Shirley: you're not to spoil these walls with dado railings, or stuff up these windows with shushi curtains,' anyone else and I'd be offended, he said, 'the rooms are small and you want to keep them simple, white walls in the hallways and up the stairs, something warm in the living room and kitchen, and plain as you can bear in the bedrooms. It'll look cramped otherwise.'

I said, 'Anyone else and I'd be offended,' (and I think I noticed a smile) but I'll do as he says. I've got my mother's taste and it's nothing special but Josh has an artistic temperament, an 'eye' as they say.

Eight, supermarket; tick, but the grocery list was separate and already thrown away. Not that there's any point in me writing that list, I don't know why I bother. Once a week I go to that store on the way round to Mum's (nine, tick) and buy much more than I ever intended or needed, but they have ways of tempting you, those massive supermarkets, built of the edges of cities where there's plenty of room to spare. Plenty of room for plenty of shelves stocked with so many plentiful things they make your eyes go squiffy. And Oliver plays up in the trolley so I have to fill it quickly. This, this, this, this and this, from every shelf down every aisle. They get through it, though, my two gannets, and I like to take my mum some treats, even though she's no good at receiving. It's only forty-five minutes from our new house (fingers crossed) to her flat, half the time it takes us from here but today she wasn't pleased to see me. Odd, cos we're close; she wasn't pleased to see Oliver – odder.

But my mum gets in these blue moods from time to time and I can't say that I blame her. When I was younger I dreaded growing up and becoming like her, so who can blame her for getting blue moods when she *is* her? She said, 'Shirley, you look dreadful. And you still haven't done anything with that hair, it looks like a bird's nest.' My hair has been a bone of contention for as long as I can remember. Bushy and unmanageable, but what can I do? I decided to ignore her. Her flat was looking particularly squalid, the sink full of washing-up that hadn't been done, her cigarette smoke showing up specks of dust in the air. I said, 'Mum, what are you going to be like when you're an old woman?' and she said, 'I expect I'll stink of piss.'

I would've offered to clear up, but you never know if she's going to be grateful or annoyed so I just said, 'Not in front of Oliver,' and she grunted. I said, 'I've brought you some things, where shall I put them?' but she didn't respond. She didn't respond to anything I told her, the house, or Christmas, or Oliver, but I went on chatting, hoping she'd join in sooner or later and when she didn't I said I'd go.

'Oh, that's just like you,' she said, 'always rushing off.'

'I'm not rushing off.'

'Always busy, always doing some stupid task that isn't worth doing.'

'Like what?'

'I don't know, ironing your knickers.' The word 'knickers' made Oliver laugh and thank god it made Mummy laugh too, and me, and then the mood was broken. We had a nice cup of tea after that.

My mum and my dad met when they were only eighteen and I was born ten years later. My dad was going to be an actor. If he'd have lived, my mother has always been telling me, he would have been the most fabulous actor, he was destined for greatness. The talent of that man, the intelligence, the looks . . . his parents used to say the same things and it didn't occur to me until recently that he had twenty-eight years to make it big, but didn't. Bit parts. Ollie likes to hear stories about him, which is lucky, likes looking at the crumpled-up photos she has of him dressed up as standard-bearer number five et cetera. 'You take after your grandad, Oliver,' she says, 'you've got his looks and his charm, you've got a big personality just like him,' but I don't like to hear her talking like this, it gives him too much to live up to. I had too much to live up to myself when I was younger and it gave me big ideas, big plans which made me unhappy. Thank goodness for Andrew who is pleased for me just to be me, fat, middle-aged and ordinary. But we stayed long enough for Oliver to have his tea (I could use that mince tomorrow, then) and when we left Mum had a smile on her face and I'd washed the dishes.

She gets at me, occasionally, for the things I do for Andrew, says I wait on him too much, says, 'Is this what your ambitions have come to? full-time wife and mother?' Says, 'Oliver won't be around forever and then your life will be empty,' but I don't think it will, and besides, it's all about compromise, marriage, it's all about finding out what makes someone happy and doing it. I could have carried on working if I'd really wanted, but when Andrew gets home from the office it brings a smile to his face to find Oliver waiting for him and something delicious wafting from the kitchen and so I gave up my job, so what? I traded in a paltry wage for a lot of appreciation. When Andrew comes home he gives Ollie his bath, puts him to bed and reads him a story while I sit at my desk. Ten, personal admin: tick. I paid the bills, I wrote our round robin and I made out a list of people to send it to. I'd better buy the cards tomorrow, only two weeks to go, Christmas post and all that. Andrew and I had chicken curry for supper in front of the telly. I made enough to freeze a load for Boxing Day (eleven, tick) and then felt too bushed to do the ironing (so I can't cross *every*thing off my list after all. Twelve, iron sheets: carry over till tomorrow). Andrew said, 'Don't bother with the ironing, Shirley, let me run you a bath,' so I did.

Six o'clock in the morning is a part of the day that I love and this is a part of the day that I love too, bedtime. I sit up in bed and run through everything I've done today and everything I've got left to do tomorrow. It's been a productive day today but I'm going to do better tomorrow. Ring Mr Petersham and take him to the house. Finish the ironing. Send off our cards. Get some presents for Andrew. What to get for Andrew? I can hear him next door in the bathroom, washing his hair and whistling. Why he has to wash his hair just before he gets into bed, I don't know. I make him put a towel on the pillow. He comes in and says, 'Good news about Josh and the house.'

'Yes,' I say, turning back the covers for him to get in, 'But he told me off about my interior décor.'

'Too bold?' he says, grinning.

'Yes.'

'You've just got a big personality,' he says, 'But I like you big,' and squeezes my bottom. Thank God for Andrew who loves me, fat, middle-aged and ordinary. Thank God for Andrew who loves me being wholly, one hundred percentedly Shirley. My hair ballooning out on the pillow, my big bones beside his smaller ones. I kiss him with my big mouth. I never thought I would be, but I'm happy. Live big, that's what I say, and dream small.

nine

I can't decide what to do this New Year's Eve. I've been invited to a dinner party, a party in a pub, a club with Garry and his mates, and a cocktail party. None of these is particularly appealing, though, I'm not sure why. I'm trying to imagine my ideal evening but perhaps it doesn't exist. I am racing through my mental jukebox: tracks I like, faces, places, what would make me feel good? what would I like to do? If you can't imagine it you can't have it, so they say. I say, piss off. But then, I can see how this makes sense.

I need a holiday, I think, I just need a break. But winter is a bad time of the year for gardeners and what with Christmas too, there's nothing going on but the rent. Granny says, 'Why don't you go to Auntie Stella's for a couple of days?'

And I say, 'You know, perhaps that's not a bad idea.'

'You could take Birdie with you,' she says, 'she'd love it. No reason why you couldn't go tomorrow,' and before I've put the phone down I've agreed to get the keys. She only lives up the road. Unlike most of my friends who have come here for work or come here for kicks or came here because they hadn't the imagination not to, I was born and raised in the city. My parents were too, their parents, and back, back, back as far as anyone can remember. So far, that our little tribe no longer restricts itself to one particular hamlet but covers the city's surface area. I have intimate access to its every sector. I have poor cousins, rich cousins, bohemian cousins, cousins on the cutting edge and all of these cousins include me. I go everywhere and everywhere I go I am an insider.

The only member of my family who ever moved elsewhere was my great aunt Stella, called Auntie Stella to her face and Mad Auntie Stella when she wasn't looking. At the age of twenty-four and still unmarried, Mad Auntie Stella collected together every penny she owned and bought a tumbledown barn in the middle of a muddy field. Three miles away from the nearest town is fairly annoying now and must have been terrible then, but she lived in it, quite happily, until she died in May last year.

I have often thought that as well as having a birthday each of us also has a deathday and I have wondered when mine is. Auntie Stella's is May the twelfth. Grandpa's, March the ninth. Granny's, bless her, can't be too far off. This is her house, the same house she's always lived in, all her married life. (My father grew up in this house, it makes me feel strange to think about that.) Downstairs in Granny's house is a dining and a sitting room, both of which she never uses. She sits in a snug adjoining the kitchen. If the wall was knocked down they'd make a decent room, but the kitchen is small and the snug is smaller and it only has two chairs, one either side of an ugly gas fire. She sits on one; since May, Birdie has sat on the other. I say, 'Are you *sure* it's a good idea to take her with me? It *is* a very long way.'

'She's looking forward to it,' says Granny, 'She can't wait to see her old home.'

'You don't think it might confuse her?'

'Not at all,' says Granny, 'She wants a proper run.'

'You won't miss her?'

'A little dog?' she says, but nevertheless she's packed a rucksack. She says, 'I've no idea what state the house is in.'

'I think I was the last one there.'

'Oh were you? Oh you'll know then. Stay for as long as you like – it's always been a special place for you,' and then there's one of those moments, that hurt and are gone; when it feels like somebody knows, like somebody's got to the heart of the matter, I say, 'Thanks, Granny,' and then I forget what it is.

I'd be surprised if I wasn't the last one there because nobody ever goes. You'd think we would, wouldn't you? you'd think we'd jump at the chance – get out, get down to the sea, at the weekend, whenever – but we don't, the city sucks us in. We may think we've our fingers on the pulse and the world at our fingers but we're very parochial, we rarely go anywhere else. There are too many entangling things, pressing things, exciting things, urgent things, fun. Even I haven't been there for four months and I'm the one who loves it best. As Granny says. End of August, beginning of September, I made an attempt to clear the garden – the roses had bolted, the grass was high, there were nettles and dandelions in the flowerbeds – but somehow it was all so beautifully fetid I just couldn't touch it. It was feral. I'm very lazy also.

Auntie Stella had a passion for gardening which I thought I had too, but I haven't, but I'm good at it. I'm not sure why, but it was always my thing, always what I was going to do: 'Look, John, Mary's made a nature table in the kitchen,' 'Mary knows all the names of the birds in her bird book,' 'When Mary grows up she's going to be a gardener'.

For someone from my metropolitan family this was as likely as 'When Mary grows up she's going to be a ballerina' and regarded with the same paternal fondness. My know-ledge of our native flora and fauna, my green fingers, were paraded in front of uncles and aunts like childish pliés and pirouettes. But somehow it stuck. Well, you've got to do something. Well, there are worse things to do.

When I get home there is still the question of what to do this evening. Lily's answer-phone message says she wants to go to the party in the pub. Garry's says, Lily has persuaded him to go to the party in the pub – earlier at least and then the club later. I ring both. I say 'I can't think I'd like to do either.'

Lily says, 'Come round. *We'll* get you in the party spirit.'

I say, 'I'm going to my aunt's house for a few days. Do you want to come?'

'What, tonight?' she says (and I suddenly think *Why not?*). She says, 'Come round.'

I do, but I pack first. I empty my fridge of food to take with me. I turn off the heating. I call my mum. I suddenly feel incredibly relieved and satisfied, strong like I've made my mind up, that doesn't happen often. Lily and Josh are smoking cigarettes at the table in their kitchen. That big pine table, that white tiled floor, that's how I'll always remember them. I say, 'You do love your cigarettes, you two.'

'It's just an excuse to sigh,' says Josh, and raises his eyes to heaven.

I say, 'I'm going up to my aunt's old house.'

'Tomorrow?'

'Well I was going to go tomorrow but I've been thinking of going tonight.'

'Why? Wait till tomorrow.'

'I really want to get out.'

'But what about midnight?'

'I'll be there by then.'

'You don't want to spend it on your own.'

'I don't care.'

'No, it would be horrid. It would.'

'It'd be okay if you didn't notice it,' says Josh. 'Spend it in transit. Then you could leave here when we leave and give us a lift.'

'Yeah.'

'No, it'd be funny,' he says, 'You'd go out on New Year's Eve, excited like everyone else, but then keep going . . .'

117

The city is spilling her guts this evening, the streets full of revellers, the roads too, it is stop start stop start for an hour before I reach the motorway. Someone sticks his thumbs up at me, as he walks past me, stuck in a jam. It is New Year's Eve, the whole world is my best friend. People in party clothes hurry in and out of off-licences, hail cabs, swing into bars, swing arms round each other, over and over like a film on a loop. But midnight passes me by somewhere on the motorway. I am surprised, actually, not to be the only car. I am not just surprised but also a little annoyed, and I realise what it is about Christmas and New Year that makes me feel so weird. Everyone's doing the same thing. Everyone *is* doing the same thing and there's something about this which faintly disturbs me. *It's worse in the city*, I think, *with the houses so close*, and then I suddenly feel very lonely, I suddenly feel very sorry for myself, as though there is a lot of fun going on somewhere without me, like I am a kiddie throwing a tantrum, then regretting it too late. But it only lasts a moment. *I am on my own* I think. But then, I am not on my own. Birdie is on the passenger seat, snoring.

You can tell she's always been an old person's dog, she has very muted emotions. She might look surprised or suspicious or aggrieved but she'd never run for cover or howl for escape. Still, I'm not sure she won't be traumatised, I would be, wouldn't you? Returning to the scene of your life, your life like it was until it changed, inexplicably, not all that long ago; your owner gone, you're not sure where, your home suddenly vanished, you, moved to a place with hardly any outside, and just as you're getting used to your life by a dingy gas fire – paradise. But only for three days. She wakes up the moment I turn off the engine, so quiet, suddenly. She sits up. She sniffs the air. She and her muted emotions can't believe she's here.

I can't wait till tomorrow. Breakfast and walks along the beach. I want to wake up having one of those moments: opening my eyes not knowing where I am, or, opening my eyes thinking that I'm still at home, and then an instant of delight when I realise that I'm not. This is my favourite place, the air, the calm, the starry sky, this courtyard, my aunt's old house; but for her a tumbledown barn. It is less of a barn, actually, more stables, built on three sides of a square. Out front there's this courtyard, out back there's the garden, then fields, then trees, then the path to the shore. The front door is right in the middle, a white wooden door, one large iron key. It always smells the same, this house, vaguely fragrant – but – it doesn't do tonight, more musty. I guess it has been shut all winter. Straight ahead is the staircase, the driftwood railing Stella made running up the wall. Birdie pushes past me, nose low, tail wagging, she turns right and I lose sight of her down the corridor. I go left, into the sitting room; I turn on the light. It looks just the same – but then – it feels very different, colder somehow, and not because I last came here in August, colder in an emptier kind of a way, as though the further it gets since Stella the more of her seeps through the plaster. But perhaps it just needs a fire. This floor could do with a sweep, I notice, this rug with a vacuum, those surfaces with a damp cloth. Their neglect offends me and not because I'm zealous about cleanliness but because it doesn't feel right here. Dust has no place here. This is my perfect place.

I walk down the corridor, through the dining room, turn ninety degrees and am in the kitchen. At the far end are the wood and wrought-iron barriers which once divided horses from each other when this was stables. Stella incorporated around them her stove, her cupboards, her table and chairs, she kept the cobbled floor and didn't build a ceiling. A frame of giant metal slats supports the roof and wall, half the roof covers the kitchen, then, half of its slates have been replaced by glass, so the kitchen wonderfully becomes the greenhouse, accessible through an arch. The kitchen heats the greenhouse, that's the idea, but the kitchen's rather cold these days and the light in the greenhouse doesn't work and something is dripping.

I'll have a bath and go to bed. No, I won't. It'll take an hour to heat the water. I'll just go up to bed. I put Birdie's cushion in its old place by the stove and give her a bowl of water and shut her in the kitchen. Upstairs, the airing cupboard is full of Stella's bedclothes, a waft of fresh laundry escapes as I delve among them trying to find her linen sheets, her patchwork quilt, the rose-and-green-striped blanket. I put my head on top of the pile and I cry, I'm not sure why.

Recently – and I attributed it to winter, the dark, drizzly city streets, the going to work in the cold – I've been finding it hard to get up in the mornings. But it lasted even when

I had no work to go to, and it lasted over the holiday period when everyone else was in the party spirit, and it's lasted today when I'm here, when there's a sea just over there and the birds are singing. I want to regain unconsciousness. Birdie can just lie down, at any time, close her eyes (sometimes not even close her eyes) and start to snore. She can fall asleep to order. I think I snore, too, so it's something we have in common. We also have in common staring.

She was a good reason to get up this morning and I went down to her kitchen prison to see how she was. It was freezing. She's not a morning person and just rolled her eyes when I opened the door and wagged the stump of her tail that wasn't snuggled under her paws. But she was only too eager when she realised we were going upstairs and she jumped onto my duvet. I crawled back underneath. Perhaps if I lie here still enough, I'll melt into the bed.

I'll have to bribe myself into getting up. I'll have to say, you can go to the kitchen and eat scrambled eggs, you can wear something cosy and a scarf and a hat, you can go for a walk, you can work up a sweat, come back and have a bath in your favourite bathroom, you can light a fire downstairs, you can cook a chicken, you can eat it in front of the telly and drink a bottle of wine . . .

Or perhaps I'll just say, you can stay in bed for as long as you like, and see what happens.

I get up at three. Twilight's threatening, the light fading behind the clouds leaves them sludgy and grey. It makes me feel guilty. Poor Birdie. What a waste of a day. I get

up and pull on the clothes I took off yesterday, grab a
coat and a hat from the hall and take her outside. There's
the air again. She runs across the courtyard sniffing the
stone troughs along the wall, inspecting the weird wooden
structure in the middle, housing an old fashioned gaso-
line pump. She climbs the steps going up the side of the
stables, going apparently nowhere. She climbs back down
again.

While the right-hand side of this house, the kitchen and
the greenhouse, is connected on the inside, the left-hand
side is not. I walk across the courtyard and open its own
front door. This bit used to be the barn, downstairs for
storing equipment, upstairs via a wooden ladder for storing
hay. Stella used it for storing her nephews and nieces and
also the household appliances she didn't want cluttering
up her kitchen. There is the chimney she put through the
middle, child-proof furnaces on either side, with heavy iron
handles that closed the flames behind a burnt-glass door.
One room downstairs is a storeroom – freezer, washing-
machine, tumble-dryer – the other a sitting room; up the
wooden ladder there is still an assortment of beds on one
side of the chimney and that grainy old bath on the other.
I walk through the storeroom, round a little corner, past
a toilet, and enter a brick 'extension'. It has ivy, not glass,
in tiny windows which run above a long shelf. It has a
hole, not a door, in the wall. These gaps look out onto a
makeshift yard hemmed in by sheets of corrugated iron.
Stella lined the sheets with apple trees, she built a path
with stones from the beach; the extension became her

potting shed, the yard her kitchen garden. I pull, out of habit, a weed from in amongst her pebbles; I notice the crop of apples is rotting by the roots of her trees. The light goes, suddenly.

Perhaps I should have gone to the party yesterday, I've felt blue all evening, uncomfortable here, uncomfortable inside my skin. But I felt bizarre on New Year's Eve, didn't I? didn't know what to do with myself, thought coming here would help. Hasn't. Where to go then? What to do? I haven't been in the mood, for a while, for anything at all . . . and now an ominous feeling, terribly large and black, perhaps I've never been in the mood. Perhaps it has all just been an effort of will.

I'm no stranger to these kind of bedtime thoughts but there's no point letting them get the better, they don't exist on their own. I wouldn't be having them if I was in company, if it wasn't so quiet and dark, if it wasn't January the first and supposedly a significant occasion, if I wasn't lying in my dead aunt's bed. They don't exist on their own. It's a human condition to wind yourself up, babies do it, cry for tiredness so much that they won't fall asleep, cry for their bottles so hard they can't drink them. You need a mother to calm you down, rub your back, kiss your face, blow on your hair; you need big arms to rock you, to lull you, to sing you a lullaby, to tell you it's all going to be okay. In the absence of these, Temazepam. And I let Birdie sleep on my bed.

She goes mad the next morning, over some poor girl in the village store, buying a loaf of bread. 'Birdie!' I say.

And the girl says, 'Oh, it's Birdie. I didn't recognise you, my darling. You've got fat!'

'She's had a hysterectomy,' I say, I notice a little crossly, 'dogs get fat –'

'I'm Ella,' she says, 'My husband farms the land by Stella's house.'

'Tom?' I ask, shocked.

'No,' she laughs, 'his son Michael.'

'Oh, his son. I'm Mary. Stella's niece.'

'Well it's nice to see you,' she says to Birdie, and to me, 'How long are you staying?'

'Until tomorrow,' I say, 'We're just going for a walk along the cliff.'

'I bet she's glad to see her beach again.'

'She is.'

She loves the beach.

Look at her there in her little dog body. I'd like to be in one, occasionally. I'd like to be able to go for a walk like that. With a wet nose. Smelling. Seeing in black and white wide-screen. Running in bare paws, not caring about the stones or the sludge splashing on my furry belly, my dog's tail wagging in the air.

It's all right for Birdie, she doesn't have to do anything apart from be a dog. What do I have to do? From the edge of the cliff I can see across Michael's fields to Stella's garden. Her lawn looks atrocious, long, the same yellowy colour as the grass his cows are grazing. I resolve to mow it before I leave tomorrow. – It's the least little thing I could do.

ten

In the end, I left the lawn till last. I rang Granny with the bright idea of tidying the garden and she said she'd pay me the going rate. Luckily I work for myself, fortunately or not I had none. 'It needs to be done,' she said, my wages could come from Stella's estate.

I thought it would only take me a couple of weeks (it's not a big garden) but one job leads to another, doesn't it? worse, one job creates two more. Auntie Stella was eighty-four when she died and she hated delegation and nothing had been touched for years. Generations of nettles had infested the flower beds, grown tall, gone brown, seeded, and in various stages of decay were rotted in a tangled mush. Brambles grew determined over walls, cut my hands when I tried to pull them up and brought up with them roses and shrubs. Most of the roses had to be chucked anyway, not fed for years, infested season on season with aphids. Not that there *are* many at this time of the year, just the odd one or two, but aphids freak me out. They are born with their babies inside them already (so it's a losing battle) and I'm jealous – they are born with their purpose intact. More than this, their babies are clones of themselves. Aphids are immortal.

The roses I could save had bolted in their search for light, looked straggly, forlorn. For three weeks I did nothing but prune. Prune and burn, prune and burn, I am expert now at building a bonfire.

After a while it was the same bonfire which never went out which I kept feeding, I liked that. I built it in the compost yard and ferried fodder in a trailer which I borrowed from Michael. I could spend an entire day up a ladder in the cold, hacking away, lacerating my hands, and come back down to notice no difference, but at least I had a whole trailer of food for my bonfire. It was an emotional moment when it finally burnt out.

There were actually a lot of emotional moments, most particularly when I caught a glimpse of the mountain ahead of me. It would go something like this: I'd be pruning and burning, pulling up and burning, pulling up by mistake and setting aside to plant back again, buoying myself up with self-manufactured enthusiasm, and then I'd take a break, come back and the wholeness of my job yet-to-be-done would suddenly present itself ... Oh my God! I'd say, Why did I take this on? Even when I've finished it'll never be finished, that's the point of gardens, like painting that suspension bridge, getting to the end, and having to start all over again. There's something about a garden that reminds you horribly of life. Everything finished is really something only just begun.

But that can be a joy, too, depending on your mood. And the good thing about being up here and not in the city is that my mood depends upon me and on no outside influence or opinion.

You get into a rhythm, you see. You have to tell yourself, I'm here, it's fine, I like it; it's like dancing. You have to talk yourself into it at first and then you just do it. Then you just are it. Dance.

I was going to add the massive pile of ash from my bonfire to the compost bins when I noticed they were all collapsing. I thought, well I should empty them anyway and use their contents to feed the beds; I thought, but before I do that I should sort out what's to stay and what's to go, I should do some digging up. It started raining then and there was nearly a moment of emotion but I reined in. I wondered if Auntie Stella lived like this? It is one thing to stay in someone's house, even over a period of years, quite another to live in it. To become familiar with all its systems, to know the contents of its drawers, to clean it, heat it, lock its doors. I have come to know Stella's life far better in the past six weeks than I ever did while she was alive. I had always thought her house had an essence of its own which, if it does, was the touch of her hand; I had always presumed that she had a passion for gardening which I didn't have. In the days when she was nimble, her garden was beautiful, diverse – an extraordinary, breathing work of art – and I'd just assumed that she woke up each day, eager to get out there. But she can't have done. She must have thought, while pumping out the pond, sweeping away the sludge, scraping off the blanket weed; she must have thought, when cutting the juniper brought her hands up in hives, when she spent all day in the rain, when she raked up the leaves from the drive only to have to rake them up all over again: bugger this! what on earth's the point of this? And only very occasionally: look at that! I did that! – How beautiful is that?

The apple trees had made amazing shapes untended, and I've left them pretty much, but re-trained the roses climbing up their trunks. I've tidied the beds, divided shrubs with a spade and re-allotted them or put them to one side. I've done the mulching and nailed up the compost bins and filled them with leaf mould and mouldy apples. Today I'm going to tackle the lawn. My deadline is: this weekend.

Last night Ella came round for a chat and found me and Birdie in the greenhouse. I was potting up spare shrubs (a result of my dividing) and I showed her the cuttings that I'm hoping will root and the seed pods I'm going to sow. She said, 'This is such a fantastic greenhouse.'

'I know,' I said, 'but look how mouldy it is. Up there. And look at all those broken panes of glass that I've just stapled over with plastic.'

She said, 'It's a shame you're not staying longer.'

'Ella!' I said, 'You said that last time and I was going the day after tomorrow, and now I've been here six weeks,' but it is a shame, I do feel it's a shame, I'd quite like to be around to see my efforts come to a spring fruition . . .

Lily and Josh are coming to stay this weekend and bringing with them Oliver, their next-door-neighbours' little boy. It's a favour; their next-door-neighbours are moving house. I've decided to go back when they do, I've thought that'd make things neat. So I've made up the beds and cleaned the bathroom and driven to the village to buy them chocolate treats. Birdie and I are going to look for sticks this afternoon, for kindling. Going 'sticking' Auntie Stella used to call it. When I was little, and even when I was big, Auntie Stella was always sending me scuttling to the woods, or scouring the paths for twigs with one of her dogs (none of her dogs was ever any help but) I loved sticking. The lining of the pockets of my coat used to get all muddy and wet and infuriate my mother. Now they get all muddy and wet and infuriate no one. I've dispensed with smart coats.

It is February and the time of the year for my favourite flowers, hellebores. Auntie Stella's are white, flecks of green or pink their middles. They look like the oldest plants on the earth, I've always thought, like the dinosaurs ate them, with their pronged leaves supported by sturdy, spreading stems. There are bulbs, too, starting to poke through the ground, crocuses coming up in the vegetable garden, wild garlic about to line the path to the shore and snowdrops nodding round the church.

There was a strong wind last night, and plenty of twigs have come down, too many to carry all at once. I leave them in bundles at the roots of their trees. Looking at them, I remember that Buddhists believe in cleaning karma, that it's a good deed to do, making things neat; I think of Adam and Eve clearing their garden; I've a sudden moment of . . . right-ness? yes-ness? Zen, perhaps – a vision of the world feeding itself, the wind blowing down branches, Birdie and me picking them up, burning them to keep us warm, returning the ash to the earth where worms will return it to soil.

The whole world is alive, I've realised since I've been here, and me, and I am a part of the world.

Not that I didn't know that before, no, but in the city never *realised*, not like it's clear here.

Fire is alive. I light one every night. There is something wonderful about a fire which negates the need for telly. I am addicted to fiddling with it once it's lit, poking around the charred bits of wood, adding twigs as carefully as the heat allows, watching the embers glow pink, fog over ashen, then glow pink again, chucking in my saved-up candle butts when it needs resuscitation . . . 'But we've got to go back,' I say to Birdie, 'you to your gas fire and I to mine,' and she looks like she understands and is vaguely disappointed (but she always looks that way, her little face anxious and concerned) and for a treat, I let her sleep on my bed.

When they arrive it's late, they got lost, Ollie's been sick in the car. 'What a trauma of a journey,' says Lily.

'I thought you lived in a graveyard,' says Josh, 'all those white lumps. And then I realised they were sheep.'

'They're Ella's and Michael's,' I say, 'the farmers next door.'

'Been making friends with the locals?' laughs Lily. They're full of stories. She's got a new man, he's been on holiday, they've both been to this new bar and that new club and a mutual friend's fab party.

'I'm so glad you're coming back,' says Lily, 'partners in fun!'

But after we've all gone to bed, I find I can't sleep. I remember those first few days after I arrived, when I felt there was a little knot of something hard in my back, anxious, acting like caffeine. I lie still for a long time, lulling myself, then give up, get up, put on my dressing gown, grab a towel, some soap, a log, some twigs, Birdie, and close the front door behind me. Oh, stars! Oh, moon! (And there's the air again.) We walk diagonally across the courtyard to the front door of the old barn. I turn on the light. Climb the wooden ladder up to the bathroom and lay a fire in the child-proof furnace. Light it, light some candles. Run a bath.

I'm rather good at drawing a bath, but I need the raw materials: a clean room, preferably; ideally a huge room, a huge room with lots of space for lots of towels; in my dreams, space for a sofa; and in my wildest dreams, a fireplace. This bathroom is from my wildest dreams and for twenty-odd years I've had plans for it. This is what I used to do when I came to stay with Auntie Stella: soak, and plan its transformation . . .

When I was at school I had a history teacher called Miss Aherne and a geography teacher called Miss Tomley. Miss Tomley was also the deputy-headmistress. She was far more threatening than the actual headmistress who was more of a fictional character, a hologram produced only on a Friday for assembly. Miss Tomley was tall (probably not as tall as I remember her, aged eleven) and had blonde hair, which, now I come to think about it, may well have been a wig. It was cut short at the fringe, parted on the left and tapered over her ears to the nape of her neck. She wore glasses and a sky-blue rollneck. She was incredibly thin and had bony, pointing fingers. Miss Aherne was smaller, stouter, of no figure at all, she had short, dark, salt-and-pepper hair. She wore beige jumpers and a faint moustache, mannish skirts with American tan tights. She was one level up. She spoke to us young girls as though we were university students, giving me a standard which I wished I could reach, an expectation I wished I could live up to. Miss Tomley, similarly, treated us as though we were undergraduates, but undergraduates at a fifth-rate college at which she, with a first-rate brain, had been forced to teach. She wished we were boys. Boys, she constantly told us, were more intelligent than girls, so much more intelligent than girls, and she should be teaching *them*, but because of her sex she'd been lumped with us. I was not aware of living in fear of either of these ladies, but I must have taken to heart the constant blow of their disappointment for I remember one school holiday coming to stay here, lying in this bath with the fire spitting behind its window opposite, lying entirely underwater apart from my nostrils, rising to the surface as I breathed in and filled my body with air and sinking again when I let it out. And when I let it out I thought *they can't touch me here* and felt entirely relieved. *They are so irrelevant here. They've never seen this bathroom* . . .

'Partners in fun,' Lily said. But it seems to me that I stopped finding it fun, such a long time ago, but was too in my life to notice.

For there's nothing much I've missed about my city life; my family, of course, my friends, entertainment at the end of a bus ride . . . but not enough to want to go back. Phone calls come less and less often from those with whom (I realise now) I only had in common a current drama, or a correspondingly disastrous love life, or a social scene – and I missed them at first, but not any more, not so I'd like to take them up again. A wonderful hush has replaced a fog of chat and gossip and opinions confusingly contradictory on subjects not worth the waste of breath. Too much, too much, too much information. I'd prefer to spend my evenings with Birdie.

But what sort of attitude is that? and what sort of place is this for a young girl on her own? and what was Auntie Stella thinking? The same thing as me, I imagine. In the past six weeks, for the most part alone, I have felt myself being stripped bare and I don't want to put my old clothes on. I don't want to put any clothes on until I know what I look like naked.

It's a beautiful day the next day. I wake to find my guests have been up for hours and helping themselves to bacon and eggs. 'Afternoon,' says Josh.

'Make yourselves at home,' I say.

'Oliver's just said he wishes he had six fingers on every hand.'

'Do you, darling? Why's that? For counting?' He nods.

'I think it's a good idea,' says Lily, 'because then we'd count in twelves instead of in tens, and space and time are all divisible by twelve – hours, days, circles . . .'

'Lily's got it into her head that we're all out of sync,' says Josh, 'that ten fingers is an evolutionary design fault.'

'It's fucked us up,' says Lily, and then, 'You didn't hear that, Oliver.'

'It's lovely here,' says Lily later, as we walk along the cliffs, 'but you must have got over it by now.'

'I'll never get over it,' I say as I look across Michael's field to Stella's garden. Her lawn looks great, neat, startlingly green next to the yellow grass his cows are grazing. It took me four days of scything, raking, clipping, raking and mowing, but look at that. I did that. How beautiful is that?

On Sunday afternoon, Michael takes us 'on safari' in his pick-up. He and Ella sit in the front, the rest of us cling to each other in the back. We're out to see a hare, a deer, a fox, a kestrel and a cow – Oliver's to point them out. The last one is easy, the other ones not so, I don't hold out much hope . . . But in the middle of a field of last year's wheat, stubbly like Gulliver's chin, Birdie jumps out of the truck and careers after a hare. Oliver laughs, ecstatic. Lily says, 'Every day's a Vietnam if you're a rabbit,' and I remember a fact I read once: Earthworms have forty percent of the same DNA as humans. Suddenly it makes sense to me. It's all the same thing, life, all the same source. And perhaps it suits me better, living here amid its myriad manifestations and not just among one kind, people.

– I could mend the greenhouse

– I could grow seeds, sell plants

– I could do people's gardens

– I could live in the barn and let the house

– there are plenty of things I could do for money, not that I'd need much money

– Birdie would love it.

– I'll talk to Granny.

'I'm not coming back', I say to Lily and Josh.

'You will be back,' says Lily as she gives me a hug goodbye. 'I give you six months.'

'Come again, won't you?' I say and she nods. Oliver's strapped in the back. Josh is driving, Lily is buckling up. They wave. They hoot. I must stand for a while looking at the space they've left for Birdie suddenly whines. 'It's all right, angel,' I say, 'We're going in now.' We turn round and go back to the house.

eleven

Just at that point where the nail leaves the confines of the finger and grows towards the air, there is a wonderful arc of skin, juicy like flesh, guiding it on its way. One on each side of each nail, two corners for every finger. Not on mine, though, not any more. The last time I had those bits of me intact – in their entirety and not just half-grown back, never more than half-grown back before they're forcibly removed – I was twelve. I was watching television. I looked down at my hands, and noticed those small corners as I never had before. They looked ripe enough to bite. They looked perfect. I put the little finger of my left hand to my mouth and its arc of skin fitted neatly between my left canines, top and bottom. Chop. Efficient as a guillotine. I moved my finger along the front of my teeth until it touched the canines on my right side. Same finger, other corner. Chop. This gave me a strange sensation of pleasure and I repeated the operation, left right, left right until my left hand had no more corners, then right left, right left, until my right hand looked the same.

My mother said, 'Colin! Stop biting your nails.'

Whether this remark was the incentive for me to continue or whether I would have done anyway – once bitten, no, once I'd got the bit between my teeth, better – I don't know, but I am inclined to blame my mother. Why not?

Although, having never wished that I didn't bite my nails, I hardly regret the start of the habit. Blaming my mother is, like the other feelings I conjure from time to time, a futile attempt to have some response to her. I still try, occasionally, to be angry, irritated, proud, affectionate, or fond in reaction to her, but these are always of my own making and utterly pointless and empty. As far as concerns my mother I remain entirely anaesthetised, and so does she towards me. Between the two of us there has never been even the remotest spark of feeling – unless indifference constitutes a feeling, which it may well do – but I don't have any regrets about this. She doesn't seem to have either.

That occasion when she told me to stop biting my nails remains in my mind vividly. Perhaps because it was one of the very few when I did something which appeared to affect her. (I know now that at that time, she and my stepfather were in the process of disentangling themselves from each other, and her nerves were unusually frayed.) I can remember where I was (in the sitting room of my stepfather's house), what I was wearing (grey sweatshirt, faded black jeans) and even the programme I was watching. It was about plants, in particular a bugleweed.

Not long afterwards, they separated. I know it was a great disappointment to her, for, having been married twice previously (and neither man being my father) she had wanted this one to last. She married again a few years later, but, that failing too, then gave in. It is not in her nature, she says.

I would describe my mother as a cold fish and wish her upon no one. Indeed I have said as much to her face. She remarked, half-smiling, 'Like mother like son,' but we are not alike. I have two loves, which seems to indicate that I could have others. That she and my stepfather were ever together continues to amaze me, he being a particularly hot-hearted and generous man. His new wife is far more deserving of him. Although, I think his love for *her* is more like relief than desperation, more fondness than the passion he had for my mother – but perhaps that's just their age.

I was the one who met him first. I was five. I lived at that time with my maternal grandparents, my mother being off pursuing her unfortunate love life. I was a shy and unresponsive child given to fits of silence which sometimes lasted days. My grandmother, fairly shy and unresponsive herself, nonetheless found my behaviour intimidating and sent me to see a psychologist. She disliked him immediately, most particularly because he was foreign. I on the other hand loved him: his accent, his cheerful room, his crayons, but mainly his interest in only me for three whole hours a week. Not that that lasted.

After a couple of months I began to think him my friend, possibly my only friend, for I was one of those annoying children who won't join in. At school I rolled pennies along the tarmac of the playground whilst the others played tag;

on social occasions I refused to go upstairs to the nursery with the toy trains and the Action Men but preferred to loiter looking hangdog on the fringes of the grown-ups. Children don't like this kind of child and neither do adults and who can blame them? But Dr Richard found me intriguing.

Once I thought him my friend he suggested my mother might attend our sessions. I was opposed and he didn't insist, but looking back now I notice he prodded me towards her inclusion gently, subtly, until one day I woke up and I wanted my mummy. My grandmother was consulted. She said it would not be easy, first of all finding her daughter (she'd had no idea where she was for months. The last thing she knew she was living with a cowboy on his cattle ranch, but a recent telephone call had informed her she'd moved to some city. No address.) then convincing her to come home and live with her parents, and, perhaps hardest of all, persuading her to go to a psychologist with her son whom she'd always considered a burden and somewhat deficient. Doctor Richard looked stern when my grandmother said this. 'The only thing this boy is missing,' he said, 'is his mother.'

So, she was found and she came – with surprisingly little hesitation. But while a person can be brought to one's side, an emotion will not necessarily follow and although my mother did come, love did not.

Not on either side which, as it happened, suited her perfectly. She had entered her parents' house nervously and in some state of self-defence, knowing her every move towards me would be noted, but she found that I made no demands that she might find unsettling: I never cried out for her, I never looked at her with imploring eyes, I never needed her in the childish sticky way we both found embarrassing. I remained exactly as I had always remained, impassive, my mother no one more distinct than any other person in my immediate life, plucked from a further world full of such people.

With the exception, of course, of Dr Richard. Our sessions with him were supposed to be for me, but soon they became for my mother and me, and this I noted neither with jealousy and regret nor with the hope that it might provide me with a more conventional family unit. My mother confided in Richard the reason she'd stayed away so long. It was not that she found me onerous and subnormal (which was her mother's interpretation and described her own feelings, nobody else's) but her lack of any maternal instinct which had inflicted a guilt so heavy that she hadn't been able to sit in the same room as the source of it, nor witness the tight figures of her parents whose disapproving faces mirrored her own internal confusion. She said she had managed to tuck this away during her absence (most of my life to that point) and hide somewhere between kidney and gut. She had terrible pains in her abdomen, spasms in her lower back. But now she had found in me a most appropriate son which, while being an enormous relief for her, was horrible for him, poor boy. She had bred a person exactly like herself, wanting no one, needing nothing.

This was not quite true but I kept it to myself and so did Dr Richard. He, interested of course in the workings of my child's mind, became whole-heartedly fascinated by my mother's, and there they had a great deal in common. It wasn't long before our visits became our favourite outings and less like psychoanalysis, more social occasions, the only ones we could go on without being nervous of our mutual nonchalance. We were encouraged to behave exactly as we wanted to behave, consider it, and then continue. In no way were we wrong, or not up-to-par, or odd. We simply were, *individuals*, (and rather marvellous ones he told us) in a world full of individuals, full of cause and effect, where no precedent should ever be set.

Exactly how their relationship moved professional – personal – physical, I've never enquired. At the time, seven years old, it was simple and obvious: when a man and a woman get on, they get married. Of course. There's no notion of the singular life in a child, it sees social units; there's no notion of time. A lifetime. A lifetime's commitment. After the wedding we left the town I'd been born and grown up in, we left my grandparents (tearful at the airport, incredibly) and we left the country. We came here – to Richard's.

Sometimes you hear people say about a place, or a house, or a person, that the moment they arrived there, went inside it, saw him/her, they *knew* they had to stay. It doesn't happen often, even when it does happen: love at first sight becomes more real in retrospect, is only true until it's over so is only true today. To me, though, it did happen. As soon as I stepped from the plane with my mother and my stepfather I knew that I should spend my life here. The air and I remembered one another; the customs officials were my kinsmen; the landscape knew my name. I felt bound by the ground at every step. This was my country! I'd a sudden vision of myself fast-forward, still here an old, old man.

In subsequent years I have asked myself how real this was and have tried to understand it. I have wanted it explained. My feelings for my stepfather were, at that time, the same as some of my mother's towards him – relief and disbelief that someone would like me to be whatever I wanted to be. But they were also similar to Richard's for her – huge and passionate, terrifying and wonderful. I keep this in mind when I consider my present predicament against my original reaction to his country. Perhaps that sense of such inevitable belonging was just an extension of what I felt for him already, a bond I urgently needed to be mutual. Perhaps it was merely the fancy of a small boy after a long journey, the tired over-running of excitement having come so far from home. Perhaps it was purely that, in the all's-mysterious, everything's-possible universe of a child, there isn't much distinction between not really and the real. Or perhaps it was fate. It was fact. Is this the place for me?

Now every reason is irrelevant. I just have to be here. It just is.

For five years I was safe. Then, in the summer between

my twelfth and thirteenth birthdays, my parents started having 'conversations'. I could hear them at night, filtering across the landing to my bedroom; I could hear them come to abrupt ends as I walked into rooms (my parents would both look up and smile); and although I couldn't hear exact words I could hear that something was being discussed, the same something, over and over again. They talked quietly and calmly, my stepfather didn't preach one thing and practise another, but there started to be a strange look on his face, not quite wild, not quite grief, not quite terror and yet all those three; there started to be a strange look on my mother's, impotence and guilt and desire to be gone. Then, there was the nail biting incident.

I started a new school that September and for a couple of months my own affairs occupied my mind, new subjects and new faces, new politics. There wasn't much time left over to notice the behaviour of my parents which seemed in any case returned to normal. But on the first night of my half-term holiday, during supper, Richard told me that he and my mother were separating. He said this was not something that had been considered lightly but which had been discussed by the two of them for several months. In fact, they'd reached their decision a considerable time previously but had not wanted to mention it while I was still so new at my school, thinking such information at a delicate time might be too much for me to cope with. He explained that my mother was unhappy. 'Not *un*happy,' she interrupted, 'just not entirely happy.'

'No,' said Richard, 'That's right.'

'I'm so far away from home,' she said, 'I haven't seen my friends or family for five years.'

I knew that she had neither friends nor cared about her family, but I said nothing.

'You do understand, don't you, darling?' she said, and did her best to smile.

'We both think,' said Richard, keeping his eyes on me, 'that it would be crazy for your mother to continue here with me, feeling as she does, when there's a chance that if she leaves she might find a different life, one in which she is fulfilled.'

This had always been his particular credo but I could see it wasn't offering much comfort. The calmness of his voice, his logic, did nothing to belie his helplessness. He looked like someone had removed his leg. I thought, 'I will have to leave him. I will have to leave here.' I think now how ironic it is that this be-true-to-yourself philosophy, that which attracted my mother to Richard in the first place, ultimately made it easy for her to leave him. Perhaps in some other age of selflessness and commitment she would have stayed with him, looked after me. Our lives would all have been different. It continues to startle me, how much is determined by the vogue of the moment. But perhaps in that other age she would have been miserable. Who knows? I wouldn't describe my mother as particularly happy in any case, even if her own person.

And actually, I didn't have to leave. It had been decided that until my mother knew where she should settle and what she would do, I should remain with Richard. She herself was staying until after Christmas ('I thought it would be nice for us to spend the holidays together,' she said but I knew that she had no rosier alternative) and so it was that on the fourth of January, Richard and I found ourselves making the long journey home from the airport as we had five years earlier. This time, I was in the front seat beside him. This time there was none of his constantly grabbing his companion's hand and pointing out some hill, some tree, some house and telling her its story. All of those stories I had remembered in much the same way as I'm sure my mother had forgotten. I said them to myself as we passed by, Richard silent and morose, I silent and ecstatic.

I knew that I was only supposed to stay with him until mother was settled but I also knew that she'd never willingly send for me, that he'd never send me away. I bided my time. I bit my nails. I have been biding and biting ever since. In the years that followed Richard was married again and by degrees had three sons of his own. I made myself an indispensable friend to his wife, an indispensable brother to his children and remain to him an indispensable link to my mother (whose occasional phone call still puts him out of sorts for days). I did well at school and pleaded that it would be academically destructive to send me to a country and a parent that I knew less well than the ones I was with. I gleaned that the strict immigration laws here would allow me to stay just as long as I was studying, so I developed a passion for architecture, the longest course I could find. College fees for a foreign student would be extortionate, but between my working every holidays, Richard's generosity and the money left to my mother by her dead parents, the sum was found. By the time I was nineteen I applied to, and was accepted by, a prestigious architectural school in the capital city.

I had never before been to the city; we lived too far away. That pins-and-needles excitement I'd felt twelve years earlier as I'd walked off the aeroplane returned, but intensified. Buses, people and buildings rushed past me, obscuring the skyline. Images crowded in one on top of the other. I felt faint. I felt out of my body. 'Richard!' I said, and he said:

'Steady. It's not forever.'

But it felt like infinity then. But it's amazing how quickly time goes. I wished that it would go slower. I tried to give myself as bad a time as possible so that it might go slower. I made no friends, I lived in the dingiest squats, I gave most of my money away, I lost weight, I was cold, I never went out, but try as I might time raced by. I was in love. I was happy.

When I had to leave, I cried. I am not aware of ever having cried before and I certainly haven't cried since. It was a strange thing, like vomiting. My mind was saying *stop, please stop* as I sobbed on my adopted family, but my body continued to purge itself, unrelenting.

Whether it was my mental state which made me detest my own country once I'd returned, or whether I could have loved it if I'd tried, like a couple whose marriage is arranged, is irrelevant. I did consider just getting on with my life, letting them go – Richard, his homeland, the city – after all, one country is pretty much the same as another in the end, one life ... But I couldn't. I went to live with my mother. She embraced me nervously and said, 'That's not my Colin,' and I thought, no, never has been, never will and began to plot my escape. I needed a plan, a good one. One has to be logical about such things. One has to be precise. It is easier to continue once one has started, relatively simple to look back and remember and then to repeat the pattern. That first step, though. That journey into nothingness. The goal distant, the way uncharted, the likelihood outweighed. It is never as simple as: do this, this, this, this and this and then you'll get what you want; more like: try, if you can, to do this, then, if it's possible, do that, and someday maybe, maybe, maybe. Life is a state of perpetual perhaps.

Is it the suspense that keeps us walking? Continual curiosity as to what might happen next? Even death is not an ending but a plot point ...

Personally, though, plot has never much mattered to me. I'd prefer to be aware of What already, and then be able to work out How. How it came to this – at last, when there was nothing to lead onto. Often, when I finish reading a book I start it again immediately. Then, knowing it all, I begin to see the way in which 'it all' was possible. I begin to make sense.

My mother and I hadn't seen each other for twelve years and while I had grown from a pup to a boy to a man, the change in her was more shocking. I wondered if Richard would love her still if he could see her. Terrible, what time does to the lovely. She was living in the same old town, in my grandparents' old house, with her old childhood sweetheart (her words) who was smaller than she, and fat, but the mayor. He got me a job at a tin-pot architects' office near to the practice where I first met Richard.

The way to get back, I reasoned, was to work hard. I am not talented at what I do, but good. Not talented because it doesn't come naturally: I've trained, I've toiled, I've tried, I'm not the best, but I am good and my god I worked hard. The hours I put in, the weekends I gave up, the new techniques I researched. My boss was thrilled and amazed, little suspecting that everything I did for him, really I was doing for me, but I didn't feel badly. I'd been a child still when I'd worked out that everyone has an agenda. For a long time I'd wanted one of my own for without one, all you are left with is other people for their sake, not yours, and that's how they get you. Even Richard had had an agenda all those years ago when, through me, he'd got to my mother. Now I did have one, now when I'd got my boss to trust me, now when I'd got him to treat me like a son, now when I'd got him to offer me a promotion I said, what I'd really like to do is to go back to the city I trained in. Just for a couple of years, I said, I'd improve my technique, I'd learn new skills, I'd come back with wider horizons, more experience, a new improved version. We could take this business places, I said passionately, and then it was easy. He wrote glowing letters, he arranged a work permit, he got me a placement, he even gave me a substantial amount of money. I shook his hand heartily when I left. I hoped I would never see him again.

The first thing I did with his substantial amount of money was buy a flat. It felt like putting down roots. It was a bit of a shell when I moved in and I had great plans for its transformation, but these have mainly been left unimplemented, superceded by my greater plan, the way to stay. I let one of the rooms to one of my colleagues at work, Jacques, a handsome fellow, passionate about architecture and with an extra-curricular obsession for his body which I guessed would keep him out of my way and in the gymnasium, giving me space to think. I guessed right. In fact it was Jacques's activities which, one Saturday morning, gave me my idea. I had considered going to the immigration office, asking for the necessary forms and applying for residency. I had reasoned that, as I'd spent most of my life here, I may have had quite a good case. But the possibility that I might be rejected closed that door to me. It felt too much like all or nothing, one chance only – if they turn me down, that's it, there'll be no other way. I had considered making myself so vital in the office that my employers might fight my corner for me, but as I've said I'm no great architectural talent, hard working, yes, but two-a-penny in this country, in this city. Then one Saturday morning, cooking eggs the way that Richard used to, a girl walked into the room and said, 'Hi'.

She was not at all self-conscious or embarrassed to find herself in some stranger's kitchen, wearing his dressing gown. She said, 'Mmm, something smells good'. She said,

'Sorry – I'm a friend of Jacques'. She said, 'My name is Tonya'. 'Groovy wallpaper,' she said.

I have never been a particular fan of the word 'groovy' or of people who use it but I let it pass because she had such a large smile on her face and a large air about her and she looked so at home and cosy in my dressing gown that I offered her half of my omelette. I said, 'The wall-paper's going.'

She said, 'Oh, no, leave it, but get rid of that horrible carpet,' so after we'd eaten she got dressed in one of Jac-ques's tracksuits and we started to pull it up. The boards underneath were dark and musty, 'a bit like your flatmate,' she said, and giggled, but all the same, she looked rather sad.

'Where is he anyway?' I asked, and she said:

'Don't you know his Saturday routine? First he goes to the gym, then he goes to play football, then he goes to *watch* football and then he gets drunk in the pub.'

'Oh,' I said. I got the feeling that I was meant to say more, but I wasn't sure what, so I didn't.

The carpet took much longer than I had imagined and I kept expecting Tonya to get bored and to leave, but she stayed. I was glad because she was much more adept than I would have been alone. If it had been left to me (not that I would have had the idea in the first place) I would have rolled up each room and then had a huge, heavy load to drag out, but Tonya cut as she went, neat little squares which fitted easily into dustbin liners. But it did take much longer than I'd expected, and by the time we'd finished I'd had the longest ongoing conversation that I'd ever had with anyone. I'd told her about Richard and my stepmother, and my three younger brothers and what they were like when they were babies, which made her laugh, and as she was going she said, 'I think this flat's going to be lovely, Colin.'

And I said, 'I hope so.'

'I must come round and see it.'

'Yes. Well, Jacques will invite you I'm sure.'

'I don't know,' she said, and there was a bit of a pause. She said, '. . . anyway . . .'

'I can't believe how much you've helped me.'

'No, I've enjoyed myself.'

'Me too.'

'You're a lovely bloke, Colin,' she said, 'I don't know. You don't like football, you make great omelettes, you know about babies, you'd make somebody a fantastic wife.'

'Would I?' I said, and she laughed.

'It was a joke.'

'Oh.'

'Well,' she said, and paused again, 'goodbye then.'

'Goodbye.'

'Yes. Goodbye.'

You'd make somebody a fantastic wife, she'd said, joking, but it gave me my idea.

Looking back on it, it was probably a mad idea, but it could so easily have worked. I often think that about life, it's full of lots of things that could so easily work, but they don't. Not for me. I thought, *What I must do to stay here is to get someone to marry me*, surely it wouldn't be so hard?

All I needed was one in a city full of millions. Just one girl who would fall in love with me just for long enough to agree to marry me. You hear about it, don't you? Whirlwind romance. Couple wed after three months. I didn't need it to last forever, just for long enough, and I was prepared to give back everything I could in return.

The method I employed shot several birds at once. First, it applied the techniques of direct marketing: if I aimed at dozens of targets I'd hit at least one. Secondly, it meant that I didn't have to change my unsociable habits or suddenly develop the confidence to go up to a girl in a bar and give her some chat. Thirdly, it ensured that my rejection would come from a distance, like an artist's, and not, like a performing artist's, to my face. By the time Jacques had returned, drunk, it wasn't only the carpet that had been torn into pieces but the sheets of paper on my drawing board, at least two hundred strips to every sheet. Upon each one I wrote my name, Colin, and my phone number. I would make a start tomorrow.

It makes me laugh now, thinking back to that evening, recalling my optimism. It makes me laugh — but you have to laugh, or so they say. They also say that if you believe in yourself and your goal you can get what you want; 'positive visualisation' they say. Fools. Not that I've given up, but if I carry on it's only because, what else is there to do? I have been failing for almost two years, I have only three weeks left. What else is there to do? But my heart isn't in it any longer, and if I carry on it's through force of habit, an addiction which no longer gives me pleasure;

it's because the means have become more definitive than the end. I am used to my routine, I find comfort in it. My name is Colin. This is what I do.

I have never felt the pull of sexual attraction as some people describe feeling it. I have never looked at anyone and thought *I'd really like to* – you know. So if I say I choose women that I am attracted to that is not quite true, but I choose women who I think are in my league, middle-of-the-road. On the underground, walking down the street, on the bus, in the supermarket, queuing in the post office, wherever I find myself next to a corresponding female, as she leaves I give her a strip from my pocket. Tens of strips every day works out on average as one date every other week, half of those one dates become two, the majority of those two become three, and once there've been three, the liaisons usually last a little while ... but never long enough.

Never long enough for there to be any spark of feeling, never for a proposal of marriage not to be completely ridiculous. But perhaps length of time has nothing to do with it. I have what most people have, the reason most people wish for love but which is, ironically, love's biggest barrier: a longing to get, via somebody else, a different life. I have an edge of desperation about me. I have an agenda, and the huge weight of my lie pulls me back from any kind of intimacy I might have found with any of the girls I've dated, had circumstances been different.

But had circumstances been different I doubt I would have looked for intimacy. I've never been an intimate kind of a person, loving only Richard and his country. The one loving me back, the other my belonging, I had never been aware of feeling lonely until I started on this search. Now, though, there is only me, there is no one to confide in, I am the only safe place. Now even the pavements tell me, even the pavements teeming with people, people like me but not like me, unaware of my dilemma, unaffected by it, even the pavements tell me how lonely I am. Different to the others I am, outside the machine; I look like them but I am not like them, not part of the family, not one of the pack and any second now I expect to be sniffed out.

It is Sunday today. I lie in bed, not moving. I don't know, any more, if I ever sleep or whether I just lie in bed not moving. Recently I have felt myself, like a machine that has been overrun, begin to slow down. It takes me forty-five minutes where it used to take me half an hour. It surprises me when I notice how slowly my legs move as they walk from one destination to another and no amount of mental effort will persuade them to hurry along. Don't they realise, time is running out? I am heavy, heavy all over. I move more slowly but I sweat more quickly. How is this possible? How can my brain be on overdrive, my internal organs be on overdrive, my sweat-glands be on overdrive but outside, I'm grinding to a halt? How can I be this exhausted and not be able to sleep? My mind and body are at odds with each other. Each takes it in turn to be the other's prison-master, its torturer. I deny you motion. I deny you rest.

I get up late. I drink a glass of wine from a bottle I keep

under a loose floorboard in the hall so Jacques won't find it. It's not good wine. I'm not sure why I hide it. I drink another, and then another. I run a bath. My skin is sweaty, my eyes are full, my fingers raw and bloody. A constant sculpture, I used to think, but it's an ugly habit, and not just the after-effects but the spectacle as well. Anxious, aggressive, self-destructive, afraid and all at once, it can't be relaxing to look at. But they are their own worst enemies. When the skin grows back it does so hard and horny and perfect to chew off. They smart, they smart! as I get under water, but it's strangely satisfying. The water hurts me but it's good for them. I tend to them. Tenderly soak them. I am mother, I am child.

I am Colin. This is what I do.

Sunday nights I work the bus route, the number 24. I met a nice girl once, on bus route 24, her name was Daisy. We went to bed a couple of times but it didn't work out. 'I just want a bit of fun,' she told me one day when I told her I liked her, so I didn't call her again. Fun's not my business. Three buses go by before I get on – there's no point getting on if there's no likely candidate, no point waiting for a maybe girl who may be waiting further down the road, you've got to start off with some cards in your hand. Three buses go by and then the fourth comes along, and when the fourth comes along there's a woman on board, sitting alone, looking out of the window. I glance at her, without letting her know that I'm glancing at her, it's a trick that I've learnt, but it looks like she's glancing at me. Is she glancing at me? Yes. I pay the driver and walk towards her. Yes. I sit on the seat corresponding with hers, on the opposite side of the aisle. Yes, very definitely, she keeps looking round and looking at me. She's watching me. She must like me. No girl ever takes this much notice of me. At the next stop I'm going to get up and give her my number. I'm going to go home and see if she calls me. She's staring and it's slightly disconcerting, I think, *perhaps she's odd*, but then, *so what?*, if she's odd so much the better. I fumble in my wallet for one of my bits of paper. I stand. I smile at her. She smiles back. I say, 'Here,' and I hand it to her, then disembark.

Walking back the way the bus came I'm thinking, *that was strange*, when somebody calls out my name. It's her. She says, 'You don't recognise me, do you?'

'The bus,' is all I manage to say, feeling slightly under pressure.

'No,' she says. 'Well, yes,' she says, and laughs, 'but – I thought it was you.'

'Who are you?'

'Lily,' she says.

'Lily?'

'Yes, don't you remember?'

'Lily?' I say again, not because I don't remember, but because the disappointment winds me suddenly . . . I think my legs keep moving, though, and I think she's keeping up with me, chattering to me and following me and all the way home. In the fluorescent light of the hallway she says, 'God you look awful,' and I find myself in tears again; bewildering tears, tears that are entirely controlled by my body. She comes in. My wreck of a flat. The floorboards exactly as she last looked at them, my duvet in a knot twisted on my bed, empty bottles sticking to the cheap formica in the kitchen – I half expect her to start clearing up but she doesn't. She swills out a dirty glass with a dribble of wine and fills it up again. She gives it to me and does the same for herself.

How long I sit there crying, I don't know. It's strangely relaxing though. Perhaps this is how Jacques feels when he sweats in the gym. Cleansed. But I find I can function, light a cigarette, take a drag, sigh it out, stare at her and all whilst those tears flow, in sheets it seems, down my face. I'm calm, utterly calm, like I haven't been in years, like perhaps I've never been because perhaps there's peace in despair and I give up. It's such a relief.

I realise I am telling her, like I would tell me, like a progress update, as though she knows the facts, about the day I landed and Richard and my 'passion' for architecture and the tin-pot office in my mother's home town; about my plan, my journey back, Jacques, Tonya giving me that stupid idea which could have worked; how it didn't, how bad I feel, alone I am, afraid, outside . . . she says, 'You're lucky . . . A lot of people wander around feeling like that but without the luxury of any excuse.' She laughs. She says, 'You are funny.'

'Funny?'

'Yes,' she says, 'Your crazy scheme,' and then, 'The irony of it is that if you'd told me all this last summer, I probably would have married you.'

'Would you?'

'Probably.'

'Why?'

'Why not?'

I stare at her. I shake my head. It seems an age before words come and when they do they're meagre. I say, 'Help.'

'I will,' she says, 'of course I will.'

'You're going to marry me?'

She smiles. She says, 'I don't think it will come to that. But, Colin, you will be allowed to stay here. We're going to do it together.'

I look at her then, and I see and feel the life that I want. It's real for an instant. In the surety of her smile, the certainty of the touch of her hand.

twelve

Reality shifts. Yesterday's givens are taken away and we take it in our stride. All the time. Nothing really matters. Shirley has moved. Only three weeks ago and the larger-than-life next-door-neighbour has nothing to do with my life to the smallest degree. Life re-morph. Next door is now full of students. From my bedroom window I can see them in their garden. Hacking down that ivy.

It needed cutting back, but trouble is, they don't know what they're doing. Chopping down the ivy but chopping down the rose as well, the rose I've trained to go under my window. And it's spring.

Lily's in the kitchen with Colin, typing on her lap-top. Goodness knows what. She's taken on an intensity of focus which I haven't seen in her before and I think it's good. She's happier. She's lost herself in something that isn't herself and, well, it's a lovely rest. So what if the whole thing turns out to be pointless? Everything's pointless. Nothing really matters, point is to do it anyway.

In my private moments, though, he does give me the creeps.

They've been trying to get him residency. Lily hired a lawyer. No, she sought out the best lawyer. Found out what documents he needed. Made lists of his requirements. Read pamphlets, wrote letters, rang him up and held his hand.

For once she didn't keep saying, 'What's going to happen in the end?' She said, 'Either he gets to stay or he doesn't get to stay. It's only books that end with marriages or death'. She who can't read a book without flicking to the end to see what happens. But perhaps that's what she's learnt about the end, it's meaningless until you've got there. And sometimes even then.

Being philosophical doesn't always pay off. Sometimes it's even more annoying when you don't get what you want when you haven't worked yourself up into a frenzy over it. Colin didn't exactly win his case, he's got to leave tomorrow. He didn't exactly lose it either. He can reapply, in time. But the last few weeks they've been nervous, excited, exultant, and tonight it's resignation. A sort of blissful, horrid resignation.

Of course for me, and to a large degree for Lily, we'll drive him to the airport, say goodbye and it'll all be over. We'll come back home.

I hoped there wasn't going to be a tearful scene. I'm not that great at tearful scenes. And I have to say there's nothing about Colin that makes me want to throw my arms round him and hug him. But as it happened a tearful scene might have been preferable to the awful nothing that was our goodbye. We drove in heavy silence, checked in, killed two hours smoking cigarettes and drinking plastic cups of coffee, glancing at the screens and going to the toilet, buying a paper and doing the crossword, and not saying anything apart from the odd, nervous 'want a fag?' 'some gum?' 'what time is it?' until the time did come, his flight was called, he said, 'I'll be all right from here,' and wandered off, not looking back. For myself, I couldn't care less, but Lily looked a bit bewildered. A little bit hollow.

In the car I notice she's crying. She puts her hand over her face and weeps until mascara runs through the cracks of her knuckles. For a while I just drive on, staring ahead, scared by the force of her misery. Then I think *pull yourself together*, fumble around to find a cigarette, light it, and push it through her soggy fingers.

She doesn't look up and she doesn't smoke. The ash on the end of the cigarette gets longer and longer and eventually drops off onto her lap. I think the butt might burn her fingers. But she takes her hands away from her face before it does and flings it out the window. She says, 'Oh my god, Josh,' she says, 'I must look a sight.'

'You do.'

'I'm sorry,' she says, 'I don't know what came over me,' and she starts to cry again. She says, 'My whole life's disintegrating.'

'No it's not.'

'But I invested so much energy in Colin, and so what now? Just another weirdo story. He didn't even say goodbye.'

I pause for a while wondering what I think. I say,

'Reasons come later, do you know what I mean? Nothing happens for a reason but you can make them up. It's all about you, how you react, what it is that *you* take and make meaningful from out of the mess.'

She doesn't seem convinced. There's a gallery nearby which I think will cheer her up. It's only a couple of rooms, a private collection, just enough to make an impression without leaving you feeling swamped. The collector was obviously interested in people for all the pictures are portraits, some ancient, the latest only twenty years old. Beside each painting is a plaque detailing the artist and the model. '"Frederick Benson,"' I say, reading, '"heir to a cotton fortune. Disinherited by his father for falling in love with a slave. He tried to eke out a living painting but died penniless in the two-roomed lodging he shared with his mistress." There she is.'

'Mmm,' says Lily.

'"Margaret Watts, great beauty of her day, she lived to the age of a hundred and two and when she died had fifty-four living descendants."'

She says, 'I just want something of my own. What's mine, Josh?'

'The memory,' I say, 'all your memories, your friends, me.'

We look at the rest of the paintings in silence, in our own heads. Lily sits on a leather couch in the middle of the room staring pointlessly at a picture of a ballerina. I stand behind her, put my hands on her shoulders. She kisses my knuckles. She says, 'In later years she suffered from rheumatoid arthritis.'

I say, 'It doesn't matter in the end. Human passion, grief, struggle – imagine the *lives* of these people – and today they're all neatly condensed into one little paragraph.'

'But is that good or bad?' says Lily. 'And anyway, at least they have a paragraph. What will I have?'

'You've got loads of stories.'

'And all of them unimportant.'

'Is that what this is about?'

'I just feel like everyone's got there, left me behind. Edward's getting married, Mary's in love with the country, Shirley knows what she wants. But me . . . I can't imagine.'

'Nor me.'

'But doesn't that freak you out?'

'No. No, not at all.'

'Why not?'

'I don't know. It just doesn't.'

'Well it's all right for you, then,' she says and I notice a tear dangling limply on the edge of her nostril. It's quickly joined by another. I say, 'Some people know what they want, and that's fine, they go for it. But for other people, people like you and me, life is a process of elimination.'

'Mmm,' she says, 'And reasons come later.'

'And you don't have to worry all about you. It's a relief when I don't.'

'Yes.'

'So don't. Don't, don't, about any of it.'

'No,' she says, 'You're right. I won't. Thanks.'

After that I ended up promising to go to Edward's wedding with her, promised her we'd have a good time. Lily is upstairs now, getting dressed and I'm staring at the invitation. It's addressed to LILY AND JOSH as though we are a couple. It gives me a bizarre sensation, not unpleasant, makes me wonder if it'll ever really be JOSH AND X and who that x might be. I can't imagine. Some people say that the human imagination is limitless, but try conceiving a colour that doesn't exist and you'll see how wrong they are. She is wearing a suit of lime green, very spring. She says, 'You'd look lovely if you didn't look so uncomfortable.' But the fact is, I am uncomfortable, I don't like dressing up. Rituals of any kind make me feel ridiculous. Like a caveman, almost, like a nerd. Stupidly self-important against the overwhelming evidence. But perhaps I can persuade myself to like a church. Their heavy smell, their stone floors smoothed by generations of genuflectors, the intensity of their atmosphere created by the intensity of thought that's gone on within them; perhaps I could like a church service. Repeating those responses in unison, those same old words that we've all known for years, comforting like nursery rhymes.

It's a morning service followed by a lunch. No dancing, thank god. There is no way to dance elegantly in this day and age, and that's fine, but not when you're in your wedding gladrags, your Sunday best. When we arrive, the church is already full. The usher, someone whom Lily knows, someone with an enormous nose and a psychedelic waistcoat, seats us in a pew next to a skinny chap with fluffy blond hair, like a chick's. He looks guilty and embarrassed when he sees Lily. She widens her eyes and looks cheeky.

I have to suppress a chuckle, because I do find it funny, Lily's disastrous life. She's always been the same, ever since I've known her, somehow on the other side of herself, finding the whole thing confusing. But she used to find it funny, too, and I'm not sure she does any more, and I hope she gets that back.

They always say, don't they, that the bride looks amazing, whether it's true or not, but today it is true. Anna is a beauty. Something Lily conveniently forgot to tell me. I whisper in her ear, 'You never told me Anna was so attractive,' and she says, 'Didn't I?' and looks at me innocently.

I appreciate beauty. It doesn't happen often. No shushing down the aisle in a meringue for Anna, she's all elegant lines in cream and gold, cream and yellow budding roses pinned along the front of her hair. ('Yellow roses for a flirt,' my mother told me once as she received a bunch from an admirer.) The man next to us continues to look uncomfortable and Lily looks straight ahead. When the service is over he scuttles off without saying a word, and I say, 'Who was that?'

'Alex.'

'Alex?'

'Yeah, you remember, a couple of years ago. I got lost in his cupboard . . .'

'Oh yes,' I say, 'I remember.'

We haven't been put next to each other for lunch so I can't see if she's having a good time, but I am. Everyone round this table finds me charming and amusing, and it's mutual. It must be the champagne. The speeches are short and witty, the food delicious. Some days, not that they come very often, everything you say comes out right, everyone laughs when they're meant to, you go away thinking 'they were nice' and know that they think that of you. Half-way through dessert I catch Lily's eye across the tables. She's laughing. We look at each other as if to signal, is it time to go home? Yes, get up, walk out, meet outside.

It is a beautiful afternoon. The sun's shining warmly. 'We could walk home,' says Lily, 'in our shirt-sleeves.' She takes her jacket off as if to prove it, and I manoeuvre her along the city streets. She has no sense of direction. I tell her I could be leading her anywhere and she says she doesn't care. I put my arm around her. Carefree, that's how I like her.

There was a hollyhock in Shirley's front yard last year; this year there are three. Huge, angry buds on them, any day about to burst forth. Lily walks on ahead, straight through the hall, the kitchen, out the French doors and into the garden. She says, 'It's the first garden day of the year.'

There's a package on the doormat which she neglects to pick up. I do. It's from Mary. I go upstairs to get out of my suit and see from my bedroom window mr faceless in his potting shed, our naked neighbours mixing cocktails in their kitchen, Lily smoking on the bench in her pants and her camisole. I whistle, she looks up and smiles. She says, 'What's the damage?' pointing at the rose bush. I say, 'You know, I think it might just survive.'

'Are they –?' she asks, indicating next door's garden.

'No sign,' I say.

'Maybe they've gone away.'

'Yes. Maybe they've gone away.'

I open Mary's parcel walking down the stairs. It's photographs. Our visit in February; Birdie on the beach; daffodils and tulips in the vegetable patch; wild garlic along the path to the sea; apple blossom on the trees in the vegetable patch; cow parsley lining the path to the sea ... There's a note too, which I read out while Lily draws a backgammon board on the paving. Pink and green chalk. Lurid today. I say, 'It matches your suit,' and she says:

'Doesn't it?'

'It wasn't that bad a wedding, was it?'

'No, it wasn't bad at all.'

'It was nice.'

'It was weird, though, sitting next to Alex. We're like strangers. We were like strangers today, didn't you think?'

'A stranger wouldn't have been so determined to ignore you.'

'No,' she says. 'Stupid git.'

She goes inside. Takes down the jar of black stones and white stones that's on top of the fridge and brings it outside. This takes me back. She sets up the board. She says, 'I kept trying to imagine us together today, I kept trying to imagine I was there with him ... there was a time! ... but, not mine, never mine.' Then, in the end, all times become 'that time', one day this time will be no more important than that time is now. You hand me the dice. You're smiling. It is June, and we will never be in love.

With thanks to:

Amanda Hornby, Benjamin Jones,
Brian Smith, Giles Smart,
Katie Collins, Josef Gardiner,
Paul Cooper, Philip Gwyn Jones,
Plum Sykes